BREAKAWAY

While Newman ran to put out the warning cones and place the blue POLICE ACCIDENT notice a hundred yards back down the road, Speers waved on the motorists who were slowing down out of curiosity. Only when they had warned the oncoming traffic of the obstruction did the two police officers cross the road to the van.

As soon as he saw the windscreen Speers knew that it had been shattered by bullets. Newman climbed up to peer in through the open window of the passenger's side. He'd seen enough accidents to harden him but this was something different.

'Oh, God!' He looked round at Speers, his face twisted by revulsion.

'What is it?'

'Come and look for yourself.'

Breakaway

Francis Durbridge

CORONET BOOKS
Hodder and Stoughton

Copyright © 1981 by Serial Productions Ltd

First published in Great Britain 1981
by Hodder and Stoughton Ltd

Coronet edition 1983

British Library C.I.P.

Durbridge, Francis
   Breakaway.
   I. Title
   823'.912[F]   PR6054.U7

   ISBN 0–340–28660–1

Printed and bound in Great Britain for
Hodder and Stoughton Paperbacks, a
division of Hodder and Stoughton Ltd.,
Mill Road, Dunton Green, Sevenoaks,
Kent (Editorial Office: 47 Bedford
Square, London, WC1 3DP) by
Cox & Wyman Ltd, Reading

1

The bleep on the alarm of his wrist watch brought Sam Harvey back to reality with a jerk. It was already nine-twenty. He would have to move fast if he was going to be at Waterloo on time. He rapidly tapped out one last sentence and pulled the sheet from his typewriter. He placed it carefully face downwards on the pile he had written since starting work at six o'clock.

His flat was on the second floor of a converted Victorian house in a quiet square near South Kensington underground station. The bow window of the large sitting-room looked out over the small park in the centre. He had placed his desk in this embrasure. It was covered now with an apparently chaotic jumble of papers and open books. There were little piles of scribbled notes, cuttings from magazines, photographs and illustrations of animals. Human beings featured only in two framed photographs. One was of Sam's mother and father standing outside the house on the outskirts of Guildford where he had been brought up. The other was of his younger sister with her Australian husband and two small children, photographed in front of their ranch-style bungalow outside Broken Hill.

The furniture of the bachelor flat was new, paid for by a surprise present from his father, who had made a shrewd investment on the Stock Exchange. The sitting-room was wildly untidy. Books had overflowed from the desk and shelves and were strewn about on the tables and chairs. Sam had a habit of taking off his coat when he came in and draping it over the back of a chair. The breakfast coffee cup had been parked on top of the TV set and a plate with the remains of butter and marmalade was on the cover of the music centre.

Sam's dress was as casual as his surroundings. He wore an open-necked shirt and a suede-faced cardigan with only one button done up. He was tall, fair and slim. Most people thought him younger than his thirty-five years. His face was alert and sensitive, the mouth seeming ready to twist up into a wryly humorous smile at any moment.

He was pushing his chair back when he saw a police car drive round the square and stop opposite. The rear door opened and a burly figure heaved itself out. Even from above Sam had no difficulty in recognising Chief Superintendent Bert Sinclair. He was surprised to see him so soon. He had only posted his letter to the Commissioner two days previously.

He had time to put the dirty plate and cup back in the kitchen before the door-bell rang.

Bert Sinclair was a good twenty years older than Sam. His hair was beginning to recede, leaving a pronounced V arrowing down towards his brow. He had heavy eyebrows and there were deep lines in his cheeks. His fingers were stubby and practical. He wore a dark suit that had stood up well to a lot of hard wear. The fatherly manner he affected could be dangerously deceptive.

" 'Morning, Sam."

"Why — hello, Bert." Sam feigned surprise, standing in the half-open door.

"May I come in?"

"Well — yes, of course." Sam stood back and opened the door wide. "But I haven't much time. I'm due at Waterloo at ten o'clock."

6

The Chief Superintendent bustled through the hall into the sitting-room, his busy eyes darting round, missing nothing.

"Ten? It's twenty-five past nine already."

"Yes. I'm meeting my mother and father," Sam said, following Sinclair into the room. "They're flying to Australia this morning. I'm taking them to the airport."

"Australia?"

"I phoned them last night. My mother could hardly talk for excitement. Still, it's not surprising. She hasn't seen Meg for six years."

"They're coming up from Guildford by train?"

"Yes." Sam looked meaningfully at his watch. "They're due in at five past ten."

"May I sit down?" Sinclair saw the hesitation on Sam's face. "Don't worry. I'll see you get to Waterloo on time."

Without waiting for an invitation he removed a couple of books from an armchair and sat down. He stared up at Sam with a puzzled expression.

A faint smile twitched the corners of Sam's mouth. "I take it you've heard from the Commissioner."

"Yes. He sent a message down via that constipated stooge of his. Sam, what *is* all this about?"

"If you've read my letter you know what it's all about. I've decided to resign from the force."

"But why?" Sinclair was unable to suppress his exasperation any longer. "Why, for heaven's sake? I know you're financially independent but you've always had your heart in your work and you're one of the youngest superintendents in the Met. Surely, at your age — "

"It's nothing to do with being independent." Sam turned

away towards his desk. "The real reason is — It's no use, Bert, you wouldn't understand."

"Try me."

"Well, if you must know, I'm going to write another book."

"What do you mean, *another* book? I didn't know you'd written one."

"I wrote it under a pseudonym. The only people I told were my parents."

"My God!" Sinclair frowned, struck by an appalling thought. "You didn't write that vitriolic crap which was published in the — "

"No, nothing like that. I've a great respect for my colleagues at the Yard. I always have. You know that." Sam hesitated before admitting a little sheepishly, "It's a children's book."

"A *children's* book?"

Sam smiled at Sinclair's amazed expression. "Yes."

There was a pause.

"You mean — a book for *kids*?"

"That's right."

The Chief Superintendent rubbed his fingers over his brow. "You've got to be joking."

"I'm not joking."

"Was it published?"

"Yes. It was published."

Sinclair sighed, prepared at last to accept the awful truth. "What the hell made *you* write a children's book? You haven't got any kids! You're not even married."

"My sister Meg was ten years younger than me. I used to tell her stories, mostly about animals. Then when she had kids of her own I began sending stories for them with my letters. Someone suggested making them into a book, so I did. It's something I've always wanted to do, and I was

8

lucky enough to have it accepted. Now, I want to do another one."

Sinclair's eyes were boring into Sam in the way that they had bored into thousands of suspects.

"You wouldn't be pulling my leg, would you, Sam?"

"I'm not pulling your leg." Still smiling, Sam took a book from a drawer in his desk and handed it to the Chief Superintendent. It had a hard glossy cover in bright colours. An assortment of animals, exquisitely dressed in modern clothes, were sitting round a table. The host was a lion.

Sinclair stared at it in amazement, then slowly read out the title. "*Dinner at the Zoo*. But this is written by Sam Kaye."

"Kaye was my mother's name, before she married Father."

Sam retrieved the book before Sinclair could delve further into it. "Bert, I've really got to be making a move."

It was ten minutes past the hour when the police car raced up to the car and taxi waiting-area outside Waterloo Station. Sam opened the door and jumped out as it screeched to a halt. With a wave to Bert Sinclair and a nod of thanks to the expert police driver he turned and dashed towards the main arrival hall.

He had no difficulty in picking out his parents. They had already come through the barrier and were standing searching the crowd for their son. A porter with a trolley bearing their suitcases was showing obvious signs of impatience. Jason Harvey was in his middle sixties but still erect and sprightly. His neat and new-looking clothes gave him a dapper look. He had retained hold of a leather document-case which was stamped with the initials J.H. It was secured by a combination lock. By contrast Hannah

Harvey, though younger than her husband, seemed flustered. Two arms did not seem sufficient to cope with her fur coat and the large hand-bag she was carrying. When she saw Sam her pink chubby face broke into a relieved smile.

Sam kissed his mother and received a pat on the shoulder from his father.

"You're late, darling," she chided him. "We were beginning to wonder if something had happened to you."

"I told her to stop fussing," Jason said, "I knew you'd turn up — eventually."

"Yes, I know I'm late. I'm sorry, Mother. Here, let me take your coat and bag. Well — how are you both? Excited?"

"Excited?" Jason commented drily. "That's the understatement of the year."

The porter had little time for their family exchanges. He began to wheel his trolley towards the taxi-rank. "You wanting a taxi, sir?"

"No," Jason told him. "I've ordered a hire-car. It should be waiting for us."

As the party emerged onto the pavement outside the main hall the door of a white Ford Granada parked across the roadway was opened. A slim leg wearing a neat shoe emerged, followed by the rest of a very good-looking girl. She was holding a clip-board in her hand and appeared to be very self-possessed as she walked across towards the Harveys. She was wearing a dark purple suit with a jacket of more than waist length and a skirt with one pleat in the front. A leather handbag was slung over one shoulder, the strap across her bosom.

She walked straight up to Jason. "Mr Hogarth?"

"No. The name's Harvey."

"Harvey?" The girl looked puzzled. She consulted her

clip-board. "Did you order a car from Brewster Bros, Hammersmith?"

"Yes, that's me. But the name's Harvey, not Hogarth."

She was obviously embarrassed and shot Sam a nervous look.

"Yes, of course." She switched on a smile. "I'm sorry, Mr Harvey. You're for the airport?" Jason nodded. "Mr Hogarth was my last passenger. I've just dropped him. If you will wait here I'll fetch the car."

"There's no need. We can walk across."

"No, I'll fetch it, sir," the girl said firmly. She sounded as if she was used to having her way. "If you will wait here."

She gave Sam a quick smile which was less forced than the one she had switched on for Jason's benefit. As she walked away across the road the eyes of both Sam and the porter followed her admiringly. Seeing his son's expression Jason raised his eyebrows at Hannah.

Hannah smiled with tolerant affection. "It's a good thing she's only driving us to the airport."

At mid-morning the hall of Terminal 3 at London Airport was thronged with people from all the continents of the world. Sam and his mother had found seats on the upper level. They were drinking coffee as they gazed down on the colourful throng below. Every now and then the boom of the loudspeakers interrupted their conversation. Hannah's face was puckered with anxiety.

"I can't imagine what's happened to your father. He's been gone at least half an hour."

"Don't worry, Mother."

"It's always the same! He always disappears just before we start a journey. It infuriates me! I remember once — "

"Here he is," Sam interrupted. Jason had come up a

staircase behind them. As he joined them he was looking irritated.

"There's a delay, I'm afraid."

"A delay," Hannah repeated, as if this was a familiar word in her vocabulary.

"Yes, they say it'll be at least a couple of hours before the flight's called."

"Oh dear! I've been dreading this."

"There's nothing to worry about." Sam reassured her. "It happens all the time, Mother."

"Yes, of course it does." Jason turned to Sam who had stood up to offer his father the seat. "Look here, old son — there's no need for you to stay. There really isn't."

"No, of course not!" Hannah agreed. "Your Father's right for once. It's just silly your hanging about here all morning."

"Well — if you don't mind I think perhaps I will be making a move." Sam was about to kiss his mother when he clapped a hand to his pocket. "Good heavens, I almost forgot!" He took out a necklace with a gold pendant. "This is for Meg, Mother. Give her a whacking big kiss and if she doesn't like it tell her that butch-looking husband of hers can wear it."

"Sammy, it's lovely!" Hannah thrust her fur coat at Jason so that she could handle the necklace.

"I'm glad you like it. I didn't know what on earth to buy her."

"It's a lovely present! She'll be delighted with it. Why don't you buy me nice things like this?"

"Because you'd only lose them if I did. That's why." Sam took the necklace from her and unfastened the clasp. He put it round her neck.

"Wear it, Mother — then you can't lose it."

"You don't know your mother," said Jason.

Sam smiled happily at his mother, who was gazing down at the pendant on her breast.

"Have a wonderful time. And send me a cable as soon as you get there."

"Yes, darling." Hannah stood up to be kissed. "We will."

"Take care of yourself, Sam," Jason commanded sternly as he shook hands.

"And you take care of yourselves."

As he crossed the hall below Sam looked up. They were standing side by side at the rail of the balcony. Behind them two Asians had already occupied the seats vacated by Sam and Hannah. They seemed very defenceless standing there amid a host of strangers. He raised a hand to wave, then turned and strode out through the automatic doors.

Chief Superintendent Bert Sinclair's office was on the third floor of New Scotland Yard, looking out over Victoria Street. It was decorated in the low-tone grey and green colour scheme which was general throughout the building. On the walls were the photographs, charts and lists of the cases that Sinclair was dealing with. A calendar with a vintage car for each month of the year provided some light relief. The desk was covered with documents. He was trying to shift some of the grinding paper-work which is the bane of every police officer's life.

He broke off at a knock on the door and turned his swivel chair round. The visitor was Detective Superintendent Norman Ferris, an officer of the same rank as Sam Harvey but older and of a more practical, down-to-earth character. Sinclair immediately put his pen down and rose.

"Well, how did it go?"

"We had an excellent lunch and Sam insisted on paying for it. But it's no use, I'm afraid. I just couldn't dent him."

"Did you tell him he's been granted a month's leave so he could think things over?"

"Yes."

"What did he say?"

"He didn't say anything." Ferris shook his head. "It won't make any difference, Bert."

"No, I don't suppose it will."

Sinclair propped himself against the edge of the desk and signalled Ferris to take the one easy chair in the room.

"How well off is Sam?" Ferris asked. "He always seems to live very well. Has he a private income?"

"Yes, he has. An uncle of his died about six or seven years ago and left Sam and his sister a fair amount of money. I don't know how much, but it was quite a windfall. The old boy was a bachelor and thought the world of Sam."

"My uncle left me a tennis racket." Ferris laughed without humour. "It needed re-stringing. I gather Sam's mother and father are on their way to Australia at the moment."

"Yes, they flew out this morning. And very nice too. I wish I was with them." Sinclair's face became serious. "These are difficult times, Norman. The Yard can't afford to let men like Sam Harvey break away."

"Well," Ferris sighed and stood up, "that's the way it goes. Looks like we can't afford to keep 'em either."

The police car was parked on an elevated siding just off one of the main roads leading south-east from London. The two constables had pushed their caps up off their foreheads and were leaning back, idly watching the traffic and discussing prospects for that evening's football matches. The staccato voice on the radio crackled continually. The two officers would instinctively respond if their own code-sign was called. PC Newman was in his early twenties and looked very youthful with his rosy cheeks and ginger hair. PC Speers was an older and more experienced officer; he had grown a dark moustache.

Both men sat up as an E-type Jaguar flashed into view, slowing rapidly as its observant driver spotted the police car. It pulled into the slow lane in front of the white van it had overtaken. The name MARIUS OF RYE was emblazoned across the side and rear of the van.

"Funny name, that," Speers remarked, slotting it away in his elephantine memory.

"What?"

"Marius of Rye." Speers nodded at the disappearing vehicle.

"Shall we go after the Jag?"

"No, leave the poor devil in peace. I reckon that Mini is more of a danger to life and limb than an E-type."

A scarlet Mini had buzzed past, its driver crowding on full speed.

"Wasn't it a red Mini that was used in the Tunbridge bank job?" Newman's sharp eyes had focussed on the number plate of the small car. He wrote it down on the pad on his knee. "Shall we check his number on the PNC?"

Newman was still young enough to enjoy putting a query through to the Police National Computer. To humour him Speers relayed the registration number to his control. The answer came back in five seconds.

"MCG 898T. Red BL Mini Clubman. Owner D. Blackmore, 17 Highbury Villas, Croydon."

"Can't be the one. Nothing about it being stolen. What's that racket? Can you hear it?"

"Yes. Sounds like a chopper." Newman wound his window down and peered at the sky. "It is! It's flying low!"

They watched the helicopter as it headed south, following the line of the road. It was soon hidden behind the tops of a clump of trees. Newman leant back and pulled a letter from his girl-friend out of his tunic pocket. He was half-way through the first page when a brief, harsh roar was wafted down the wind.

"What the hell was that?"

"Sounded like a machine gun to me," Speers said.

"Let's move."

Newman stuffed the letter away rapidly, started his engine up and switched on the blue light. He swerved out into the traffic and gave the Rover full throttle. With siren going he forced a way past the other traffic till he had built his speed up to 95 m.p.h.

It took them less than a minute to reach the scene of the incident. The red Mini was parked awkwardly at the side of the road. Dennis Blackmore was standing beside it, waving his arm at the police car. As it braked to a halt just past the Mini, Speers saw the white van lying on its side half in and half out of the ditch. Its wheels were still turning. Its route to the side of the road was etched by black tyre marks and a trail of broken glass.

Newman and Speers jumped out. Newman opened the hinged rear door of the Rover while Speers went to speak to Blackmore.

"What happened?"

"I don't really know." Blackmore was still shocked and bewildered. "I was just catching up on the van when this helicopter went overhead. I saw him lose height and hover just ahead of the van — I mean, keeping pace with it.

16

There was a man with a gun in the open doorway. I could see his black beard. He fired a burst at the van — the din was deafening. The van was all over the road and I had my hands full trying to control my own car. Aren't you going to see if anybody's hurt?"

"When we've put the markers out," Speers told him calmly. "We don't want another accident, do we? One's enough. And keep back off the road, sir."

While Newman ran to put out the warning cones and place the blue POLICE ACCIDENT notice a hundred yards back down the road, Speers waved on the motorists who were slowing down out of curiosity. Only when they had warned the oncoming traffic of the obstruction did the two police officers cross the road to the van.

As soon as he saw the windscreen Speers knew that it had been shattered by bullets. Newman climbed up to peer in through the open window of the passenger's side. He'd seen enough accidents to harden him but this was something different.

"Oh, God!" He looked round at Speers, his face twisted by revulsion.

"What is it?"

"Come and look for yourself."

As Newman climbed down Speers took his place and stared into the van. The driver had been crushed into the corner behind his seat by the steering wheel. His head was smashed by bullets and blood was gushing from his shattered chest. Speers could tell however that he was surprisingly old and well-dressed to be driving a commercial van. The passenger was a woman. There was little blood on her. Just a neat hole in the side of her head. Her body had collapsed on top of the driver's but she was still gripping the fur coat which had been on her knee. The gold pendant hanging from a chain

17

round her neck had fallen sideways onto the lapel of her jacket.

Mrs Carr surveyed Sam's flat with satisfaction. It was looking a great deal tidier than when she had come in that morning. The pile of dirty dishes had been washed and put away. The bedroom and sitting-room had been hoovered, dusted and tidied. She had not laid a finger on the desk, though she had itched to get her hands on it. Sam had warned her that on no account was she to touch it.

She was a motherly sort of person, well over sixty, with a pleasant face and comfortable figure. She did not really need the money but she was happy to oblige a nice gentleman like the young Superintendent. You could pick up a lot of interesting tit-bits of information when you worked for a police officer.

She had put on her hat and coat and was getting her things together when she heard a latch-key in the door and Sam came in. He had a folder of drawings under his arm.

"Hello, Mrs Carr. I thought you'd have gone by now."

"I've only just finished doing your bedroom."

"I'm afraid I left it in rather a mess."

"No more than usual, sir. There's several letters for you. I put them on the desk. I haven't touched it, of course."

Sam crossed the sitting-room, picked up the sheaf of envelopes and quickly riffled through them.

"There's a cablegram here. When did that come?"

"About an hour ago. Maybe less."

Mrs Carr hovered in the hall, as Sam ripped open the envelope. Ever since the cable had arrived she had been curious to know what it was all about. She saw Sam's expression change as he read it.

"Not bad news, I hope."

Sam lowered the telegram and stared out of the window, his face bewildered. "It's from Meg — my sister in Australia. My parents weren't on the plane when it landed."

"Whatever can have happened?"

"I can't understand it. I took them to London Airport myself."

Sam read the cable again as if it might tell him something different.

"Is there — is there anything I can do, sir?"

"No. No, thank you, Mrs Carr."

She hesitated, then picked up her bag and went out through the hall. He heard her open the door and then the murmur of voices. She was back a moment later, followed by a very worried-looking Bert Sinclair.

"There's a friend of yours to see you, sir."

"Why, hello, Bert! Come on in. What brings you here?"

Sinclair had stopped uncomfortably in the doorway. Behind him Sam could see Mrs Carr's apprehensive face.

"Sam. I'm afraid I'm the bearer of very bad news."

"Bad news? What do you mean? What kind of — ?

Sam broke off. His eyes had registered the black leather document case in Sinclair's hand. It was secured by a combination lock and he could see the initials stamped on it.

"Drink this. It'll make you feel better."

"Tell me again, Bert. Tell me what happened."

Mrs Carr had reluctantly departed and the two men were alone. Sam was sitting in an armchair, his head in his hands. Sinclair had to lift his hand and place the fingers round the glass. He went back to the side table to measure a second tot of whisky for himself. He felt he had earned it.

"We don't know what happened. Not exactly. One minute the van was on the road, the next minute a helicopter appeared and — according to a young man called Dennis Blackmore who was driving a Mini — someone in the helicopter fired a number of shots and the van suddenly veered — Look, Sam, come and spend the night at my place and we'll talk about it later. I may even have more information by then."

"No," Sam shook his head vehemently. "I want to talk about it now." He looked at the whisky in his hand but did not drink it. "Please, Bert. I'll be all right in a minute, I promise you."

"Okay — but drink that first. Then we'll talk."

Sam nodded and then with a sudden gesture knocked back half the whisky.

"What was the name, Bert? The name you mentioned — the name on the van?"

"Marius."

"Marius?"

"Marius of Rye."

"I've never heard of them. Who are they?"

"We don't know. We were hoping you'd be able to identify them. They're not in the phone book and the local police haven't the slightest idea who they are." Sinclair took a sip from his glass, thoughtfully watching Sam. "You've never heard them mentioned?" Sam shook his head. "You're sure of that?"

"I'm absolutely sure. But tell me — what was in the van?"

"Nothing. It was empty. Whether there's something concealed in the chassis or not, I wouldn't know. Our people are taking a good look at it, we'll know more about the van later." Sinclair moved round to the front of the chair Sam was sitting in. "Sam, when you said goodbye to your mother and father, at the airport, how did they seem?"

"Excited — but otherwise perfectly normal."

"There was never any suggestion that they might call the trip off?"

"Good heavens, no!"

"What happened to their luggage?"

"I imagine it was checked in and eventually put on the plane." Sam raised his head. "Although I must admit I didn't actually see it checked in."

"Why was that?"

"There was a queue at the desk and I went upstairs to make a phone call. We met in the lounge about ten minutes later."

"Then what happened?"

"Father discovered the plane was delayed and since there seemed very little point in my hanging about the airport, I said goodbye."

Sinclair nodded. He moved across to the desk and picked up the document case which he had put down on it.

"This case was in the van; it's got your father's initials on it so I imagine it belonged to him."

"I gave it to him," Sam confirmed. "It was a birthday present."

"Does that mean you know the combination?"

"Yes — unless it's been changed."

Sinclair handed Sam the case. "Would you open it, please?"

Sam closed his eyes to recall the mnemonic which would give him the number of the combination lock. He laid the case flat on the floor and spun the six bevelled rings. The lock sprang open. One by one he removed the contents of the case and placed them on a coffee table. There were the two passports belonging to Jason and Hannah Harvey, a pair of sunglasses in a mock leather case, a copy of Sam's book *Dinner at the Zoo*, a set of keys, a box of indigestion tablets, a well-used pipe and tobacco pouch and a large unsealed envelope.

Bert Sinclair picked up the envelope and turned it over and over in his hand. It bore no inscription.

"Have you seen this envelope before?"

"No."

Sinclair opened the flap and withdrew a large glossy photograph. There was nothing else in the envelope. He studied the photograph expressionlessly, then turned it round so that Sam could see it.

It was a well-focussed black and white shot of the white van. The inscription on the side stood out even more boldly than in real life. MARIUS OF RYE.

It was two days since the double murder. Bert Sinclair was seated behind his desk, refilling his pipe for the fourth time that day. Norman Ferris was standing with the photograph of the van in his hand, reading and re-reading the inscription as if it could tell him something. Sinclair was on the Marius of Rye case full-time now, assisted by Superintendent Ronald Bellamy. All material which did not relate to it had been taken from the board on his wall, to be replaced by scene-of-crime photographs, shots of the white van from all angles, a large scale map of the area, an aerial photo of the section of road where the shooting had taken place. On his desk were the results of the enquiries which his team of detectives had made at all the bases from which helicopters could be hired, a report from the Home Office Forensic Laboratory on the van, a list of possible owners from the National Vehicle Licensing Centre at Swansea, eye-witness accounts from residents in the area who had seen the helicopter or heard the shooting.

The helicopter had vanished without trace, in just the same way as the van had materialised out of thin air.

"We just don't seem to have got anywhere in the past forty-eight hours," Ferris said with exasperation. "Who the devil are these people, Bert? Marius of Rye! If they're a firm we should know all about them by now."

"No-one knows anything about them. No-one's even heard of them. And the van's revealed precisely nothing."

Ferris put the photo back on the pile on the desk. "Has Bellamy come up with anything?"

"You know Bellamy." Sinclair waved a hand at the papers on his desk. "He spends most of his time writing memos! The man's memo mad. I suspect he sends his wife a memo before climbing into bed with her."

"I don't know why on earth he was put on this case. He and Sam have never seen eye to eye about anything. Have you spoken to Sam recently?"

Sinclair struck a match and concentrated on getting his pipe going satisfactorily before he answered.

"I dropped in on him this morning."

"How was he?"

Sinclair shrugged. "He seemed all right, considering. He was on his way to Guildford."

"Guildford?"

"That's where his parents lived."

"It's a frightful business." Ferris shook his head sympathetically. "Must have been one hell of a shock to him."

There was a knock on the door. Superintendent Ronald Bellamy came in. The two other men carefully controlled their faces and avoided catching each other's eye. Bellamy was tall, with a dark, taciturn and humourless face. He had the slightly aggrieved expression of a man who tries very hard yet never receives the rewards he knows he deserves. He was carrying a memo sheet in his hand.

"Excuse me, sir," he said, glancing nervously at Ferris. "I was about to send you this memo, when I thought I'd better — " His anxious expression brightened for a moment. "We've finally come up with something, sir. The van was stolen from a garage in St. Albans."

"When was it stolen?"

"About a week ago. It belonged to a dry cleaning firm called Drake and Waters. They've got a fleet of vans. This one was in for routine service. It was due to be picked up the day it was stolen. Needless to say, neither the garage nor the firm have heard of Marius of Rye."

"Pennymore" was in a road of detached houses about a mile from the centre of Guildford. It had a slightly American appearance, because the front gardens were open onto the road. A clause in the lease prevented owners from erecting high wooden fences or growing tall hedges.

Sam Harvey had driven down from London in his 1973 Porsche 911E, waiting till the worst of the morning rush-hour was over before starting his journey. He turned in onto the U-shaped drive and stopped dead opposite the front door. He got out, closed the door and stood leaning on the roof of the car. The place looked very closed and empty. The garage at the side of the house was locked and though the curtains at the windows had not been drawn the house had the expressionless appearance of an empty property. Obviously the papers and milk had been cancelled.

Sam dreaded the moment of entering the house. His eyes swung round towards the tree to whose stout branch his boyhood swing had been fixed. He became aware that he was being watched from the garden of the house next door. A middle-aged but still comely woman was standing by a rose-bush with a pair of secateurs in her hand.

24

Realising that he had seen her she hesitated a moment before raising her hand in a slightly embarrassed greeting.

When Sam opened the front door he expected to meet the resistance of a pile of mail, but the door swung open freely. He did not close it behind him as he went across the hall. The door of the sitting-room was open and reflected sunlight poured through. On the threshold he paused, reluctant to enter. Unbidden, the memory of this room as it had been on the day of Meg's wedding came flooding back. He thrust it away. Someone had murdered Jason and Hannah Harvey. Sentiment and emotion would not help him to find out who.

The room was unnaturally tidy. His mother's sewing and embroidery things had been put away. The magazines were neatly stacked and the books had been put back in the shelves which occupied the whole of one wall. There was a faint smell of furniture polish in the air. He crossed to his father's desk. It was a fine nineteenth century piece with a top of tooled green leather. The incoming mail had been placed in a neat pile on the blotter.

He was sorting it into two heaps when he heard a footstep crossing the hall. He turned to see the Harveys' next-door neighbour coming into the room. She had taken off her gardening gloves and left her secateurs behind.

Margaret Randell had a good figure, dressed well and went regularly to the hairdresser. She used a rinse to keep her hair dark and emphasised her well-shaped fingers and nails with scarlet varnish.

"Mr Harvey? I don't think we've met. I'm Margaret Randell." She had a pleasant voice with no trace of an accent. "Your parents asked me to look after the house whilst they were away."

"Yes, of course." Sam banished his gloomy thoughts and gave her his most friendly smile. "They told me."

"There were several letters. I put them on the desk."

"Thank you. I've just been looking through them."

"Mr Harvey — " She came further into the room, trailing one hand along the back of the sofa. "I don't know what to say to you. When I read about your mother and father I was so upset, so utterly bewildered — "

"Yes, I'm sure you were, Mrs Randell." Sam interrupted her a little brusquely. He could not face a display of emotion, whether genuine or contrived. "When did you last see my parents?"

"The day they were due to leave for Australia. I drove them into Guildford, to the station. If I remember rightly they said you were meeting them at Waterloo."

"Yes, that's right."

"And — did you meet them?"

"Yes. I went to the airport with them."

"What happened at the airport?"

"Their flight was delayed — at least, so I was told. They insisted on my saying goodbye to them. At the time it seemed the sensible thing to do." Sam was staring out through the french windows. The well-kept lawn was already beginning to look tufty. "Later they — Well, you know what happened. You must have read the papers."

"But didn't your sister contact you? Surely when they failed to arrive — "

"My sister received a cable from my father, sent from London Airport, saying that my mother was down with the 'flu and that they'd be arriving a week later."

"A week later?" Margaret Randell's eyes had widened with curiosity. "Then why go to the airport?"

"I don't know." Sam shook his head. "I just can't imagine why they went there."

She moved across to the mantelpiece and began to re-arrange the china ornaments which had been replaced unsymmetrically by whoever had dusted the room. He knew that she was watching him in the gilt mirror above the fireplace.

"Mr Harvey, I only met your parents about a year ago, when I moved down here. I'd had a pretty awful time. My husband had left me and — Well, I won't bore you with that sordid little story, but I would like you to know that I had a great respect and affection for your parents. They were very kind to me, at a most difficult period of my life. I'm a rather private sort of person, Mr Harvey, and yet somehow your mother and father always seemed to make me feel — " Her voice trembled a little. "I shall miss them both dreadfully."

"Thank you," Sam said, a little embarrassed by this declaration.

"If I can help you in any way — " she turned round and looked at him with slightly moist eyes, " — any way at all — please don't hesitate to let me know."

"That's very thoughtful of you. I appreciate it." She gave him a smile and went towards the door. "Mrs Randell — "

"Oh, please," she said, turning, "do call me Margaret."

"Margaret — er — did my father, or my mother for that matter, ever mention the name of Marius to you — Marius of Rye?"

"No." She shook her head and wrinkled her brow. "They didn't. But the number of times I've been asked that question during the past twenty-four hours!"

"By whom — reporters?"

"Yes, there's been quite a crowd of them down here, asking questions. And my goodness, are they persistent!"

"I'm sorry if they've worried you."

"I'm not complaining. Please don't think that," she said, a note of anxiety in her voice. "It's just that I'm a — well, I'm a rather private sort of person. Any kind of publicity is anathema to me. Which is silly, I suppose. They've got a job to do like anyone else. Marius of Rye? That was the name on the van?"

"Yes."

"Your parents never mentioned that name. I'd have remembered it if they had done, I'm sure."

Sam nodded and gave her the smile of reassurance which she appeared to need. She was waiting for him to add some comment when the telephone on Jason Harvey's desk began to ring. Margaret Randell made a gesture towards it and tactfully withdrew.

Sam was reluctant to take the call. He was afraid it might be some acquaintance of his parents who had not heard about the tragedy and he would have to explain what had happened all over again.

He picked up the receiver and instead of giving the number just said, "Hello."

"This is the overseas operator," a crisp voice said. "Hold the line, please, I have a call for you."

There was the usual series of clicks and squeaks and then the agitated voice of a man came on the line. He had a strong mid-European accent.

"Hello? Hello . . ."

"Who is that?"

"Can you hear me?" the caller shouted, his voice so loud that Sam took the receiver a few inches away from his ear.

"Yes, I can hear you. Who is it you want?"

"I have a message for Mr Hogarth."

"Mr Hogarth?" Sam repeated the name, trying to remember where he had heard it recently.

"Yes. May I speak with Mr Hogarth, please?"

"I'm afraid you've got the wrong number."

"What number are you?"

28

"This is Guildford 31885."

"Guildford?" The caller sounded very surprised. "I'm very sorry. I'm afraid I 'ave got the wrong number." The disconnection came immediately after the last word.

Sam contemplated the buzzing receiver with distaste, then replaced it on the stand. He went to the desk and sat down in the chair, resigning himself to opening the letters addressed to his parents. He inserted the ivory paper knife in the first envelope but before he had time to withdraw the sheet he became still. Then he turned his head to stare at the silent telephone. He had remembered where and when he had heard the name Hogarth.

2

The garage of Brewster Bros was in a street off Hammer-smith Broadway. An upward-sweeping canopy protected the four petrol pumps from the rain. One sign advertised four-star petrol. Another indicated that Barclaycard, Access and Visa credit cards were accepted. Several cars were parked on the forecourt, prominent among them a scarlet Lotus Elite. On the plate glass of the showroom a notice in large letters proclaimed "SELF-DRIVE. UNLIMITED MILEAGE."

Sam drove past the petrol pumps and parked his car beside the Lotus. He gave it an admiring glance as he closed his own door, then headed for the entrance to the showroom. He was half-way to it when it swung open. As far as the man who came out was concerned Sam might not have existed, for he went past without so much as a glance in his direction. Sam, whose mind recorded an instinctive mental photo of everybody he saw, quickly took in the sullen mouth, the close-set eyes, the balding head, the hands that were quickly thrust into trouser pockets. He was a badly-preserved thirty-year old of a type Sam instantly distrusted.

Sam did not turn before pushing through the showroom door. If he had he would have seen the other watching him with intent interest before opening the door of the Lotus.

The showroom contained a wide range of new and second-hand cars. It appeared at first to be empty. Then Sam located the office in a bay opening off the main display area. A youngish man was seated at a desk, sorting through papers. Sam had a chance to size him up as he approached across the strip of carpet that bisected the showroom. He was dressed in a light blue suit, widely striped shirt and a tie with a motif of golden leaves. He wore buckskin shoes and had a ring on one finger.

He glanced up as Sam came into his field of vision.

"Good afternoon. Can I help you?"

"Mr Brewster?"

"That's me," the co-proprietor said cheerfully. "Peter Brewster."

"I'm Detective Superintendent Harvey."

"Yes, I know. I recognised you."

"I'd be grateful if you could spare me a few minutes, Mr Brewster."

Brewster pushed his chair back and stood up.

"Yes, of course, but I've already been questioned by a colleague of yours. Chap called Bottomley."

"Bellamy," Sam corrected him, straight-faced.

"Sorry. Bellamy."

"When was this?"

"Early this morning. He was here when I arrived. Not exactly a charmer, your Mr Bellamy."

"He means well."

"You could have fooled me."

Sam suppressed a smile.

"This is more in the nature of a private enquiry, Mr Brewster."

"I understand. Go ahead. If I can help you I will." He waved a hand at the upright chair facing his desk. "Take a seat."

Sam sat down and leant forward. "Who was the young lady, Mr Brewster, who drove my mother and father to the airport?"

"Her name's Foster. Jill Foster."

31

"Is it possible to have a word with her?"

"Not at the moment, I'm afraid. She's at lunch. She went late." He shot his cuff to look at his watch. "She'll be back about three o'clock."

Seeing Sam hesitate, he added, "If it's urgent you'll find her in that little Italian place round the corner."

"Thank you." Sam made no move to get up. "Mr Brewster, when Miss Foster first saw my father at Waterloo, she addressed him as Mr Hogarth."

"Mr Hogarth?" Brewster seemed genuinely puzzled.

"Yes."

"I can't imagine why she did that. She knew his name — she had full details of the booking. We give our drivers full instructions before they leave here."

"Apparently her previous passenger that morning had been a Mr Hogarth — "

"Her previous passenger?"

"Yes. And that's why I'm here. I'd be grateful if you could give me some information."

"Miss Foster had no other passenger that morning," Brewster interrupted firmly. "She picked up the car at about nine-fifteen and drove straight to Waterloo."

"Are you sure?"

"I'm quite sure."

Sam contemplated him with the friendly, slightly amused expression which so often disarmed those whom he was questioning. Brewster met his eyes levelly and only looked away when a foreman in a white coat came up to hand him a sheaf of forms clipped together. The foreman favoured Sam with a nod and a smile before returning to the repair shop.

"How long has Miss Foster been working for you, Mr Brewster?"

"Jill's been with us about four or five months. And very

32

reliable she is. I wish I'd a couple more drivers like her. She's easy on the eye, too, which is a plus so far as most of our customers are concerned."

"Did Superintendent Bellamy question Miss Foster?"

"Yes, he did. And I might add he was a great deal more civil with her than he was with me."

"That's because you're not so easy on the eye." Brewster grinned and Sam stood up. "Thank you, sir. I won't take up any more of your time."

"That's all right. If there's anything else, you know where to find me."

When Sam had gone out of the showroom doors Peter Brewster walked across to the plate-glass windows and watched him as he went past his car towards the corner where Drysdale Villas joined Hammersmith Broadway.

The Bella Napoli was a small but cosy restaurant. The proprietor had done his best to give it an Italian atmosphere. There was a large and excessively colourful wall painting of the bay of Naples, executed by some friend with artistic ambitions. Chianti flasks hung from the ceiling. A huge net, garnished with papier-mâché lobsters and crabs, was draped across one wall.

The waiter looked up with some concern when he saw Sam come in from the sunlit street. It was almost three o'clock and he had already taken the bill to one of his last customers. The arrival of Sam meant goodbye to his chance of seeing the Arsenal v Juventus match on the TV. But instead of sitting down Sam went towards the attractive girl at one of the corner tables. She had paid her bill and was just closing her handbag and preparing to leave.

She looked up when she realised that someone was coming right up to her table. Her surprise at seeing Sam was evident, but she showed no alarm.

"Miss Foster — "

"Why, hello." She smiled, looking up at him. The muted beat of the cassette player continued in the background.

"They said at Brewster Bros I might find you here. May I sit down?"

"Well — "

"I won't keep you long."

"I'm due back at work at three o'clock and I mustn't be late."

"What I've got to say will only take a few minutes."

"Very well." She closed her handbag and put it down on the upholstered bench seat beside her. Sam's easy and friendly manner was disarming. His casual style of dress made him seem much less formidable than Superintendent Bellamy. With her observant woman's eyes she noted the long fingers with their well-kept nails, the hastily combed hair recently tossed by the wind, the notebook and pen in the top pocket of his cardigan.

As Sam pulled back the chair across the table her expression changed and she said, "I was deeply shocked to read about your parents. I just couldn't believe it."

"Miss Foster, since you're obviously in a hurry I'll get straight to the point. When you met my father, at Waterloo, you addressed him as Mr Hogarth."

"I did?" she said, very surprised.

"Yes. You asked him whether he'd ordered a car from Brewster Bros and when he said yes you replied, 'just wait here Mr Hogarth.'"

"I don't remember saying that."

"You don't?"

She shook her head with apparent sincerity. "No, I'm afraid I don't."

"But — surely you remember. You consulted the list

you were carrying and said, by way of explanation, that Mr Hogarth had been your previous passenger."

"I'm sorry, I have no recollection of this. In fact you're mistaken. I only had one journey that morning, which was to take your mother and father to the airport." Sam had his forearms on the table and was looking at her with his steady, faintly amused expression. "If you don't believe me I suggest you have a word with Mr Brewster. He makes all the appointments."

"I've already had a word with Mr Brewster."

That did not surprise her.

"And what did he say?"

"He confirms what you have just told me."

"Well — there you are!" She smiled disarmingly. "Surely that satisfies you. Why question me?"

"I've just come from my parents' place at Guildford," Sam said, his expression hardening. "Whilst I was there someone telephoned and said he had a message for a Mr Hogarth. It struck me as being a rather strange coincidence that you should have called my father by the same name."

"But I didn't." She was groping for her handbag again. "In any case, that doesn't sound very important to me."

"Doesn't it, Miss Foster?"

"No, I frequently dial the wrong number and ask for the wrong person."

"Do you? That does surprise me."

She met his gaze challengingly and Sam realised that she was attractive without being beautiful. Her dark hair was parted in the middle and swept back over her ears. The style emphasised her high cheek-bones. For some reason she kept her hands constantly busy, moving the plates and cutlery on the table, folding and unfolding the bill, plucking at her sleeves or the lapel of her dark suit.

She said coldly, "Is that the only reason you wanted to see me?"

"No, not the only reason. Had you met my father before?"

"I'd never seen either of your parents before I picked them up at Waterloo. Mr Harvey, do you know what I think?"

"No, please tell me," Sam invited, showing polite interest.

"I think you must have heard the name Hogarth somewhere else. Perhaps a colleague of yours mentioned it, or you saw it in a newspaper, or read it in a book."

"Is that what you really think?"

"Yes, it is."

"Well — shall I tell you what I think?" Sam stared at her for a moment. Neither his face nor his tone changed. "I think you're lying, Miss Foster."

The smile was suddenly gone from her face. Her eyes half closed and the carefully assumed air of confidence crumbled. Then she abruptly stood up, slung the handbag over her shoulder and marched out of the restaurant.

This time he did not turn to admire her walkaway, but sat examining his hands, and the shiny little indent on the inside of his right index finger.

Sam was hungry when he got back to his flat. It was half-past three and he had not eaten since breakfast. He went into the kitchen, made himself a cheese sandwich and returned to the sitting-room. He stood in front of his desk, re-reading the hand-written first draft of his next chapter. When the last of the sandwich had been devoured he sat down, still chewing, picked up his pen and began to write.

His mind back among the animals which had become as

real to him as the humans in his life, he was completely unaware of the passage of time.

The ringing of the doorbell startled him and brought him back to the present. With a frown of annoyance he put his pen down. He was rubbing the spot where it had pressed on his second finger as he crossed the hall to open the door. The bell was sounding again before he reached it. The man whose hand was pressing it looked startled when the door opened. He removed his finger as if it had been burnt, then quickly collected himself. Despite his lack of assurance there was a prosperous look about his new overcoat, the check trousers of his suit and the slim rolled umbrella. He wore gold-rimmed spectacles.

"Mr Harvey?"

"Yes."

"My name is Randell. Walter Randell. My wife, Margaret, lives next door to your mother and father in — I beg your pardon, forgive me, I mean, she lives next door to where — "

"What can I do for you, Mr Randell?" Sam interrupted, to spare him further embarrassment.

"I'm sure you're a very busy man, and indeed a very worried man these days. But I would like to talk to you, Mr Harvey, if you could possibly — "

"Yes, of course. Come along in."

"Thank you. That's very kind of you."

At Sam's invitation he hung his coat and umbrella in the hall, then, obviously not happy with the adjustment of his glasses, preceded his host into the sitting-room.

"I don't know if you've actually met my wife — "

"Yes, I have. Please sit down. Can I offer you a drink?"

"Thank you, no," Randell answered somewhat primly. "You say you've met Margaret?"

"Briefly," Sam said, non-committally.

"What was your impression of her?"

"My impression of her?" The question, put so early in the conversation, was surprising. "Since you ask — I liked her."

"People do like her, at first." Randell took the indicated chair. "She has an air of sincerity and a superficial charm which works wonders. Mr Harvey, you'll probably think this visit of mine is something in the nature of an impertinence because, quite frankly, I'm here for one purpose and one purpose only. To warn you."

His eyes swung round to Sam as he said this. Sam could not help smiling at the melodramatic statement.

"Warn me? Against what?"

"Against my wife."

"Why do you wish to warn me against your wife, Mr Randell?"

"Because she's not at all what she seems to be."

"Are any of us what we appear to be?"

"I don't think you quite understand." Randell's tone implied that he was disappointed in Sam. He readjusted his spectacles. "Margaret talks, by which I mean she gossips. She tells lies. She even invents stories, just to impress people. At the same time she has a habit, a rather disconcerting habit, of saying, 'I'm a very private sort of person.' Which she definitely is not! Not by any stretch of the imagination."

The vehemence in the man's voice was embarrassing.

"Mr Randell, what exactly is 'bugging' you?"

"Bugging me?" Randell bridled.

"Yes. If it's the conversation I had with your wife you can put your mind at rest. She told me precisely nothing about you. Your name wasn't even mentioned."

"I'm not interested in what my wife may, or may not have told you." Randell stood up. "She's told so many lies in the past about our marriage, our relationship, that I'm quite immune to that sort of thing. I simply came here to warn you. To warn you that sooner or later, whether you like it or not, Margaret will become involved in your affairs."

"What exactly do you mean by that?" Despite himself Sam was becoming less inclined to take the warning lightly.

"I think you know what I mean. I'm referring to recent events, Mr Harvey. To what happened to your mother and father. Believe me, I know that dear wife of mine. The temptation will be too great for her. She just won't be able to resist getting involved in some way or other."

The two men looked at each other for a moment.

"Well, thank you for the warning."

"And thank you for listening to me." Randell had gone back to his pleasant tone of voice. "I expect you think I'm very odd, talking about my wife like this."

"We're all odd, Mr Randell. In some way or other."

Randell took out his wallet. "Let me give you my card. You may wish to get in touch with me at a later date. If only to say, 'How right you were!' "

Sam had made friends with the assistant at the local library. Soon after nine the next morning she rang him to say that the reference book he had requested was in and she was holding it for him.

Mrs Carr was due at half-past nine. She only had a key to the Yale lock, so when he went out he did not fasten the mortice lock. It was a fresh, crisp morning so he decided to walk to the library. He needed to clear his head after working until two in the morning. The walk took him ten minutes in each direction and he was back by twenty-five past.

He was leafing over the pages of the book, checking over

39

the illustrations, as he climbed the stairs to his front door. Automatically, he groped in his pocket for the key. When he prodded the Yale lock with it the door swung open under his hand.

"Mrs Carr?"

There was no reply, no sound of hoover or running water. He put the book down on the hall table and walked slowly into the sitting-room, his hands ready. It was in a state of wild disorder. The books had been hauled from the shelves, the cabinet had been opened and its contents dumped on the floor. The cushions had been dragged off the chairs and settee. Worst of all his desk had been ransacked; the pages he had left neatly piled were scattered, half of them on the ground.

Expecting to find the same chaos he went to the bedroom. He had only just time to observe that it was still apparently undisturbed, before he saw the form lying face down between the door and the bed. Cautiously, in case this was some kind of trick, he approached and turned the head sideways. For once the slightly petulant expression had gone from Bellamy's face. It was replaced by a fixed rictus of agonised surprise. Luckily his tongue had not obstructed the passages. He was breathing.

Sam went straight to the telephone, dialled 999. Ignoring his letter of resignation he pulled his rank and called for an ambulance — emergency.

Ronald Bellamy recovered consciousness as the vehicle raced along the Cromwell Road, siren screaming and blue light flashing. When a superintendent of police gets mugged all the stops are out.

He suddenly clapped a hand to the side of his head and winced. "What's happening?"

"You're in an ambulance," Sam told him from the berth opposite.

"I was in your flat." Bellamy tried to sit up but the ambulanceman gently eased him back. His speech was still indistinct. "Hell of a mess. Been searched. Remember going into the bedroom — "

"Someone crowned you. Did you see anybody?"

"No. God! My head's splitting."

They were all thrown sideways as the ambulance took a corner.

"What were you doing in my flat?"

"Wanted to talk to you. I'm on the Marius of Rye job. Wanted to ask you about your parents."

Bellamy's brain was rapidly becoming clear.

"Where are you taking me?"

"To hospital."

Again Bellamy tried to rise. "Not hospital, for God's sake! Don't let the doctors get their hands on me. I'm all right, just a crack on the — "

"You may have concussion, perhaps even brain damage," Sam told him. "Anyway you need a check-up. How did you get into the flat?"

"Door wasn't properly closed. Thought, 'That's funny'. I went in and saw the place all upside down. Obviously been searched. The bastard must have been behind the bedroom door. I know, don't tell me! Never enter a room without checking behind the door!"

"I think he's talked enough, sir," the ambulanceman said. "You never know with these head cases. Till the doctor's seen him it's better not to — "

To be on the safe side the doctor decided to keep Bellamy under observation for twenty-four hours — despite Bellamy's protests. Sam rang Bert Sinclair at the Yard to tell him what had happened.

"Searched?" Sinclair repeated. "Do you keep valuables in your flat?"

"They weren't after valuables."

"How do you know?"

"Bert, I've been a police officer for long enough to — "

"All right, then what were they after?"

"I'll be able to assess that better when I've had a chance to examine the place more carefully. Getting Bellamy to hospital was first priority."

"I'll send a police car to take you home," Sinclair said crisply. "Be at the hospital's main entrance. And ring me when you've had time to check your place over."

"Oh, Mr Harvey!"

The expression on Mrs Carr's face was more of sorrow than anger. She had been tolerant of Sam's untidiness but the disorder when she had come in that morning was really too much.

"Oh, my God! You've tidied it all up!"

Sam sighed, accepting the inevitable. He tried not to look frustrated.

"Well, I've done my best. I said to meself he's been looking for something he couldn't find and then gone out in a rush. I thought I'd better put it to rights, but it's taken me so long I haven't had time to do any cleaning — "

She had replaced the cushions on the chairs. The cabinet doors were shut, though the Lord knew whether he'd be able to find anything in there again. The books were back in the shelves. In time he would be able to re-arrange them. But his desk —

"I'm sorry you had all this trouble, Mrs Carr," he said, gazing in despair at the piles of paper, typed and hand-written all mixed together. It looked neat and tidy. It would take hours to recreate the familiar chaos in which everything was ready to hand. He decided not to tell her about the intruder or Bellamy's unfortunate accident. It could only alarm her, perhaps even frighten her out of coming again. "Do you think you could make us a couple of cups of your nice coffee?"

They were in the kitchen drinking the coffee when the doorbell rang.

"Could you see who that is, Mrs Carr?"

"You're not expecting any visitors?"

"No. It could be the post. I am expecting a book."

Sam stayed in the kitchen while she went to the door. He frowned as he heard the murmur of voices continuing even after the door had reclosed.

Mrs Carr came back to whisper, "There's a lady to see you, sir."

"Damn! I'm not going to get any work done this morning."

"I had to ask her in, sir. She says she's a friend of yours."

"I'd better talk to her." Sam put his coffee down and went through to the sitting-room.

Margaret Randell had dressed in a manner which she thought suitable for London. Sam did not know enough about furs to tell whether the coat she was wearing was genuine mink or not. She was holding a large carrier bag. It was of plastic but of better quality than most, with a draw-string to close the top.

"Forgive me for intruding like this," she said, "but something very important — "

"I'm glad to see you, Mrs — Margaret. Won't you sit down?"

"I was going to phone you and then I realised I had to come up to Town anyway so I thought it might be a good idea if I called round."

"It was a very good idea." Sam returned her smile. She had a way of trying to hold his eyes, as if there were some secret they both shared.

"I don't usually drop in on people without warning."
She was still standing by the settee, choosing to ignore his
invitation to sit. "I'm a very private sort of person myself,
so I realise only too well — "

She put the carrier bag down on the settee and unfastened
her fur coat.

"I'm delighted to see you again," Sam assured her.
"Won't you take your coat off and sit down?"

His eyes had rested only briefly on the carrier bag; but it
was long enough for him to read the name emblazoned on
the plastic. MARIUS OF RYE.

3

She was still watching him as he looked up. Though his face had not revealed anything he knew she had sensed his reaction to the carrier bag.

"Where did you get that?"

"This is why I came here, why I wanted to see you," she said earnestly. "Something happened last night, something you ought to know about."

"All right, Margaret, tell me about it. But first, come and sit down." Seeing her hesitate, he added: "I was just going to have some coffee. Will you join me?"

"Thank you." She gave a sigh of relief, reassured by his friendly manner. "I'd love a cup of coffee. That's very kind of you."

Sam went to the kitchen door.

"We'd both like some coffee, Mrs Carr. There's no hurry." He turned back to his visitor who had crossed to the settee.

"Did you come up from Guildford this morning?"

"Yes, by car. I drove up."

He pulled up an easy chair to face her.

"Now just relax and tell me what this is all about. Take your time."

"I — I haven't been sleeping very well, not for several days now."

"I'm sorry to hear that."

"I wake up early in the morning, very early. Usually about three o'clock. Sometimes I read, sometimes I get up and make myself a cup of tea. This morning I woke a little later than usual, about a quarter to four. I went into the kitchen and was just about to switch on the kettle when I heard what sounded like a car drawing up outside. I looked out of the window and, sure enough, there was a car parked near the house next door. Your father's house. I stood watching it for a little while and then to my amazement, a boy climbed out of the back of the car. He was wearing a blazer and was carrying what looked to me like a parcel or a bag of some kind. He walked up the drive — limping slightly — unlocked the front door, and let himself into the house."

In the slight pause Mrs Carr could be heard preparing the coffee.

"Into Pennymore, my parents' house?"

"Yes."

"This happened at a quarter to four this morning?"

"Yes."

Sam realised he had been staring at her intently.

"Are you sure it was a boy you saw?"

"I'm quite sure. A boy of about twelve or thirteen. I stood for a little while watching the house. Then suddenly the boy reappeared. He crossed the lawn, climbed into the car, and the car drove away."

"Who was driving the car?"

"I'm pretty sure it was a girl; but it's still fairly dark at that time of the morning."

"But you saw the boy quite clearly?"

"When he walked up the drive, yes. He passed by my kitchen window. I was bewildered, I just didn't know what to do. You see, your father made a point of telling me there were only two keys in existence — yours and the one he gave me. In fact, he emphasised, in the nicest possible way, that he didn't want anyone — other than you and I — to go into the house. In the end I decided that the most sensible thing for me to do was to find out whether the boy had actually taken anything. I went all over the house. I looked in every room. So far as I could tell there was nothing missing and nothing had been disturbed. Then, just as I was about to leave, I saw this carrier. It was on the shelf in the hall, near the little window. I don't know why I didn't see it in the first place. I must have walked past it just before I switched the hall light on."

"You think the boy put it there?"

"I'm sure he did. This is what he was carrying."

Sam nodded at the carrier.

"Marius of Rye. You realise that was the name on the van, the van in which my mother and father were found murdered?"

"Yes, I know. I realised that as soon as I saw it."

"Was there anything in the carrier?"

"Yes, there's a folder with some sketches in it."

"Sketches?"

"Drawings. Rather nice ones."

She loosened the draw-strings of the carrier bag and took out an A4-sized manilla envelope. Sam rose and stretched out his hand. The envelope had a cardboard backing to prevent it from being folded. The flap had not been sealed. He took out three large pencil drawings. They represented houses in a Kensington square not far from his own flat. He recognised The Boltons, SW5. The sketches were only rough outlines but they were obviously the work of a professional.

"I think they're very good, don't you?"

"Yes," Sam agreed, "I do. I take it you've never seen them before?"

"No, never. I don't understand it. Why should a boy deliver these to your father's house at four o'clock in the morning?"

"I don't know. I can't imagine why." He glanced from the sketches to her puzzled face. "You say the boy was about twelve?"

"Twelve or thirteen."

"And had a slight limp?"

"Yes."

Sam pointed to the carrier bag.

"Have you told anyone else about this? About what happened this morning?"

"No. You're the only person who knows about it."

"Then do me a favour, Margaret. Please don't mention this to anyone else."

"If that's what you want," she said, looking up at him with serious concern, "then of course I won't."

He replaced the sketches in the envelope and put them back in the carrier bag, then sat down again.

"I imagine you must have seen a great deal of my mother and father during the past twelve months?"

"A great deal. Quite apart from the fact that we were neighbours we were very good friends. I told you, they were very kind to me after Walter — after my marriage broke up. Your parents were two of the nicest people I've ever met." She pursed her lips and shook her head. "Why they were murdered like that, I just can't imagine."

"Neither can I. But I intend to find out. I've got to. For my own peace of mind if nothing else."

"I can understand that. I only wish I could help you."

"I'd like you to answer one or two questions, Margaret. They may seem unimportant to you, even irrelevant, but — "

"Please!" she entreated him. "Ask anything you like."

"Did either of my parents, at any time, mention the fact that they'd visited Rye?"

"No, never."

"Did they ever introduce you to anyone who might have come from that part of the world?"

She reflected for a moment, then shook her head. "I can't think of anyone."

"Does the name Brewster Bros mean anything to you?"

"Brewster Bros? No. Who are they?"

"They're a car rental firm in Hammersmith. My father used them from time to time."

"I'm sorry." She gave a faint smile, disappointed at her failure to provide him with the answers he needed. "I've never heard of them."

"A girl called Jill Foster works for Brewster Bros, it was Miss Foster who drove us to the airport. You've never heard of her?"

"Jill Foster? No, I'm sorry. I'm afraid I'm not being very helpful."

"That's all right. Not to worry." Sam decided to try a more general line of approach. "Now tell me, did you ever see anything, or hear anything, while you were with my parents which puzzled you in any way?"

She shook her head, and her brow wrinkled as she searched her memory.

"Well," she said hesitantly, "there was one small incident."

"Tell me about it."

"It's to do with my husband. You haven't met Walter so it's difficult for me to — Well, about three months ago Walter came to see me. There'd been an argument about money, about a joint bank account which we both — Anyway, just as he was leaving we saw your father standing outside of Pennymore. He was apparently saying goodbye to a friend of his. I'd never seen the man before but Walter obviously recognised him. When I asked Walter if he knew the man he snapped, 'Yes, I know him! And his bitch of a wife!' Later, just out of curiosity, I asked your father who his friend was, but he didn't tell me. He was terribly evasive, which was quite unlike Jason. I don't know if that's any help."

"You said just now that I'd never met your husband. Well, I have met him. He came to see me."

"Walter did?" she said, obviously startled.

"Yes."

"Why should Walter want to see you?" Her bewildered expression gave way to one of anger. "My God, I know why! He warned you, didn't he? He warned you against me! I don't know what he said, I can't imagine what the bastard dreamed up, but I bet every penny I've got that's what happened! I'm right, aren't I, Sam?"

"Yes, you're right, Margaret."

"That always happens." She groped in her handbag for her handkerchief. "Every time. It never fails. The moment I make friends, become fond of anyone, he — He even tried to turn your mother and father against me!"

"Why should he want to do that?" Sam asked mildly, humouring her.

"Because he's Walter! That's why."

Mrs Carr chose that moment to come in with the much-delayed coffee. She put the tray down on the low table without looking at Margaret Randell.

"I've brought you some biscuits, sir — in case you'd like some."

"Oh — Thank you, Mrs Carr."

On Sam's desk the telephone started to ring.

"Excuse me." He waved a hand at the coffee as he got up. "Please — do help yourself."

As he picked up the instrument Margaret Randell was lifting the lids of the jugs to find out which contained milk and which coffee.

50

"Sam, it's Bert. Are you alone?"

"No."

"Which means we can't talk?"

"That's right."

"Can you drop in my office some time this morning?"

"Eleven o'clock?"

"Make it twelve. Then we can go out for a drink."

"I haven't changed my mind, Bert, if that's what you want to talk about."

"I know you haven't changed your mind, you stubborn son of a — It's about the Foster girl. We've got the information you asked for."

"Oh, I see. Thank you."

"Twelve o'clock?"

"I'll be there."

Sam had told Margaret Randell that for his own peace of mind he intended to find out who had murdered his parents. It did not indicate any wavering in his decision to give up police work. He knew he had been a good officer without Sinclair telling him. His rapid promotion was proof enough of that. Nor was it the sheer hard work which deterred him — the continuous grind, the squalor and sordidness of so many of his cases, the hostility at times of an uncomprehending public. In one sense he was a late developer. Or, more true to say, there was an aspect of his character which had developed late. Basically he was an idealist, sensitive by nature and with a strong creative urge. Recently he had become more and more aware that this conflict between the methodical police officer and the imaginative writer had to be resolved. And once he had made his decision he was not about to go back on it.

He found Bert Sinclair sitting behind his desk in shirt-sleeves. His jacket had been hung over the back of a chair.

His trousers were held up by a magnificent pair of scarlet and yellow braces. Two of the old-fashioned elastic armbands prevented his shirt cuffs from riding down his rather short arms. He waved Sam into an easy chair and reached for his pipe.

"Before we discuss Jill Foster, I'd like to hear about yesterday afternoon. Was anything taken?"

"No, I don't think so. The flat was searched, but so far I haven't missed anything."

"Have you any idea who it was?"

Sam shook his head.

"So you don't really know whether he found what he was looking for or not?"

"No, I'm afraid I don't. How is Bellamy, by the way?"

"He's back in his office, but he looks a little shaken." Sinclair waved his match vigorously to douse the flame, then deposited it among twenty others in the ashtray. "Sam, what's your opinion of the incident? Do you think it's connected with this Marius of Rye affair, or was it just an ordinary break-in?"

"I hardly think it was an ordinary break-in. If it was, why didn't he help himself to something?"

"I imagine Bellamy disturbed him and he took fright."

"That's possible, I suppose." Sam shrugged. "Tell me about Jill Foster. What did you find out about her?"

Sinclair leant forward and picked up a sheet covered with the notes he had made in his neat, copperplate hand.

"Her full name is Jill Lucy Foster. She's an only child. Both her parents died when she was thirteen and she was brought up by an aunt and uncle, a Mr and Mrs Tedworth. They live in Ipswich. She left home when she was seventeen and for a time shared a flat with a girl called Rachel Dawson. She now lives on her own. She's had four jobs since she's been in London, all with garages or car hire firms. I've got a list of them. According to Miss Dawson she's mad on cars, crazy about them, thinks and talks of nothing else. Apparently her one ambition in life is to drive in the Monte Carlo Rally."

"Let's hope she makes it," Sam said dryly. "What about boyfriends?"

"There doesn't seem to be any. So far as I can make out she just falls in love with cars. At the moment she's having it off with an XJ12 Jaguar."

Sam laughed. "How on earth can she afford to run a Jag?"

"I don't know how, but apparently she does. She's been with Brewster Bros", he checked his notes, "a little over four months."

"Is that all the information you've got on her?"

"No, not quite all." The Chief Superintendent noted the disappointment in Sam's voice, but he was keeping his surprise up his sleeve. "Two years ago she was arrested for shop-lifting."

"Shop-lifting?"

"The usual Oxford Street story. She walked into one of the big stores and helped herself to fifty quid's worth of stuff."

Sam shook his head with a worried frown. "I don't know why, but — I find that very difficult to believe, Bert."

"Well — there you are." Sinclair tossed his notes across the desk to him. "The details are all there."

"Did she deny the charge?"

"Vehemently, but she didn't get away with it. They gave her a six months suspended sentence. It's all there."

Sam picked up the sheet of paper. He was reading through the notes when a uniformed sergeant knocked on the door and came in.

"Excuse me, sir. Mr Corby's arrived."

"Mr Corby?"

"Yes, sir. He telephoned last night, sir, just as you were leaving. Insisted on speaking to you personally."

"Oh, that chap! I remember. What's he like, Sergeant? Sounded a bit of a crank to me."

"It's difficult to say, sir. He could be a screw-ball. On the other hand, he seems very sure of himself."

"All right, send him up." As the door closed Sinclair stood up and began to put his jacket on again. "I don't know whether this chap's a nut or not. God knows we've had our share of nut cases during the past two days. Believe it or not, we had twenty-two calls yesterday morning from people claiming to have seen the name Marius of Rye. One chap even went so far as to say he'd seen it on a hearse. Every damn call was a time waster."

"What did this man Corby have to say?" Sam asked over his shoulder.

"He telephoned last night just as I was going to a meeting. He said he had some information about the Marius affair and he wanted to talk to me. I didn't know whether to take him seriously or not. In the end, and more or less to get rid of him, I said I'd see him this morning."

"Did you ask him what his information was?"

"He wasn't prepared to tell me over the phone. Just as I was ringing off, he said, 'I'm not a crack-pot, Superintendent, if that's what you're thinking.' Which, of course, was precisely what I was thinking."

Sinclair had got his coat on and adjusted his cuffs to the correct length before the sergeant returned, escorting his visitor. The latter was a plump little man with a fleshy face, an eager expression and darting eyes. Though he had started to go bald on top he was only just into his forties. He was carrying a small valise.

"Mr Corby?" Sinclair advanced to meet him.

"That's right, sir," the little man said effusively. "Leo Corby."

"I'm Chief Superintendent Sinclair and this is Detective Superintendent Harvey."

Corby only glanced at Sam before nodding. "I know who this gentleman is. I've seen his picture often enough recently." His quick-moving eyes flicked back to Sam. "I'm very glad you're here. Because I think I've got the answer to a question you must certainly have been asking yourself during the past few days."

"I've been asking myself a lot of questions during the past few days." Sam gave him his quizzical half-smile. "Which one have you got in mind?"

"I'm referring to your mother and father, sir," Corby was staring at him, his eyes for once steady.

"I rather imagined you were."

"And what happened to them after you took leave of them at London Airport."

"Do you know what happened to them?" A hard edge had come into Sam's voice. Bert was watching Corby's profile intently.

"Yes, I think I do. In fact, I'm sure I do. They were picked up by someone."

"At the airport?"

"Yes."

"Did you see them being picked up?"

"No. Well — yes — yes, sort of — " Corby switched his valise nervously from one hand to the other. Sam and Bert exchanged an impassive glance.

"Please — sit down, Mr Corby," the Chief Superintendent invited.

"Thank you." Corby sat down nervously on the edge of a chair and placed his valise on his knees.

"Now," Bert said in a humouring tone, "supposing you tell us exactly what you know about Mr and Mrs Harvey."

"I don't know anything about them. Except what I've read in the newspapers. In fact, to be honest, I wouldn't be here now if it wasn't for my wife."

"Your wife?" Bert's voice sounded faintly incredulous.

"Yes, it was my wife who made me telephone you. If I'd had my way I'd simply have taken the film back to the shop and played hell with them. I said to Betty, that's my wife, 'once you get involved with the police — ' "

"What film?" Bert broke in, halting the flow of words.

Gratified at the effect he had made Corby put on the expression of a conjuror about to produce a rabbit. He opened the catches of his valise, took out a cine film cassette and put it on the desk. As Bert gave Sam a look which cast doubts on the sanity of Corby, Sam moved forward to pick up the cassette.

"What is this film?"

"It's a film of your mother and father, leaving London Airport."

"Leaving London Airport?" exclaimed Sam. "Are you sure?"

"Of course I'm sure!" Corby expostulated.

"Who took this film?"

"I don't know."

"You don't know?" Bert repeated, unable to keep the exasperation out of his voice.

"Of course I don't know!" The little man swivelled round to face this other questioner.

"Well — how did you come by the film?"

"By mistake. The idiot in the camera shop." Abruptly Corby stood up. His face was still a foot below those of the two detectives. "Look, I don't know about you two, but I'm a very busy man and I just haven't got time to waste.

Before we go any further, don't you think you ought to take a look at this?"

He pointed to the cassette in Sam's hand. Sam raised his eyebrows at Bert. The Chief Superintendent crossed to his desk, picked up the internal telephone and began to dial a number.

The film projection room was two floors down from Detective Chief Superintendent Sinclair's office. It was a smallish room with no windows and was equipped for lectures with slides, TV video-recordings or film. A blackboard for the use of lecturers stood on the raised dais at the far end, and there was a high desk with a back-projector. Four rows of chairs faced the retractable screen.

It had been lowered now. Sam and Bert were sitting in the back row of seats with Corby between them. In the row in front sat a detective-sergeant with a notepad on his knee and beside him Superintendent Bellamy. A patch of hair had been shaved from Bellamy's head so that a dressing could be attached to the place where his skin had been broken. He had insisted on reporting back for duty, which was bad news for everyone he came in contact with. He was unreasonably irritated by the apparent failure of the projectionist to get the film running.

"Why do we *always* have these hold-ups?" he complained, half turning his head. Bert winked at Sam and Detective Sergeant Hunter had to hide his smile.

"Ready whenever you are," a cheerful voice called from the cubicle at the back. The projectionist had been waiting for a cue to start.

Bellamy gave an exclamation of outraged exasperation. Hunter turned round, grinning, to call out: "Okay, Fred. You can go ahead."

The lights were put out. After a series of white flashes

and jerky frames the film began. Sam, leaning his forearms on the back of the empty seat in front of him, watched intently. He could not really believe that he was about to see his parents again, yet felt a strong sense of apprehension.

The first pictures were evidently 'establishing' shots to make it clear that the scene was London Airport. The images were unsteady and he guessed that they must have been taken through the window of a moving car. After some minutes the car appeared to slow down and the picture became steady. Sam recognised the area outside Terminal 3. The sun was shining and to judge by the angle of the light it was about three in the afternoon.

As the camera focussed on the entrance to the main hall Sam could hear the heavy breathing of Bert Sinclair two seats away. The only other sound was the whirr of the projector. It was eerie to watch a film with no sound track.

Most of the people taking luggage through the automatic doors were entering the hall. Those coming out were nearly all free of encumbrance. Then Sam stiffened. He had recognised the couple who had emerged, each of them heaving a heavy suitcase and at the same time trying to cope with their other belongings. He recognised his parents. They looked tired and frustrated. Hannah had put on her fur coat so as to have her hands free.

The camera followed them as they crossed the roadway, dodging cars and taxis, and reached one of the long islands where cars may stop momentarily to put down passengers. As they stepped onto the raised kerb a Jaguar XJ12 slid to a halt beside them. The driver was a woman. As she opened the door and stepped out she was facing the camera. She was wearing a light blue shower-proof coat and a scarf to match.

"Is that the Foster girl?" Bert said.

"Yes." Sam did not take his eyes from the screen. "That's Jill Foster."

Jason Harvey was obviously not surprised to see Jill Foster and the Jaguar. He gave her a curt nod and immediately went to the boot of the car, which was open. He loaded the luggage into it, while Jill opened the rear door for Hannah. Then he slammed the lid and, with his document case still in his hand, got in beside his wife. As a traffic warden loomed up Jill Foster quickly resumed her place in the driving seat. The Jaguar moved away from the kerb, the camera following it till it disappeared in the direction of the tunnel leading out of the airport.

Suddenly the screen went dazzling white. From the cubicle came the clatter of the finished reel. The overhead light was switched on. Sam blinked and let out a long breath.

Bert took one look at Sam, then turned to the huddled figure of Corby.

"Thank you for bringing the film, Mr Corby," he said, carefully playing it cool. "Now tell us about it. You say it was given to you by mistake?"

"Yes, I deal with a camera shop called Surrey Snapshots," Corby said, very pleased with himself. "It's run by a chap called Naylor. Whether he owns it or not I wouldn't know."

"Where is this camera shop?"

"It's in Shepperton. About a week ago I asked Naylor to develop a film for me, one I'd taken on holiday."

"Where on holiday?"

"In Spain. The wife and I returned from the Costa Del Sol — Costa Del Sol, you can say that again! — about ten days ago."

Corby's ebullience faded. Bellamy had turned round and was contemplating him balefully.

"Go on, sir," Bert prompted.

"To cut the story short, I dropped in the shop yesterday

59

morning and Naylor, the idiot, said my film was ready and handed me the film you've just seen. Later, when I got home, I showed the film and my wife nearly passed out with excitement." He glanced at Sam. "She'd just been looking at some newspaper pictures of your mother and father and, of course, she recognised them."

"Was anyone else with you when you showed the film?" Sam still found it hard to credit what he had just seen.

"No, only my wife."

"Go on, Mr Corby," said Bert.

"Well, that's about it. I wanted to take the film back to the shop but Betty wouldn't hear of it. She said the first thing I had to do was get in touch with Scotland Yard."

"You have a very sensible wife, Mr Corby," Bert assured him.

Corby was a little doubtful about that. "So they tell me," he said vaguely.

"You say you always deal with this particular camera shop?" Bellamy challenged him.

"Yes."

"What exactly is the procedure?"

"Procedure?" Corby was resentful of Bellamy's hectoring tone. "What do you mean?"

"I mean just that. What exactly is the procedure when you deliver a film to Mr — Naylor, did you say his name was?"

"He tells me when it will be ready and I pick it up," Corby stated primly. "That's the procedure."

"But doesn't he give you a ticket? Isn't there some means by which your film can be identified?"

"No. He used to give me a ticket but he doesn't seem to bother nowadays. Not with me anyway. I don't know about other customers."

"What's this Mr Naylor look like? Describe him."

Sam was only half listening to Bellamy's questions and Corby's answers. He was still bewildered by the shock of seeing his parents driving away from London Airport at the very time they should have been airborne on the way to Australia. That vivid visual impression of them alive and well had suddenly brought it home to him that they were dead, that he would never see them again.

"He's in the late thirties, I suppose." Corby put his head on one side. "Got a damn silly moustache which makes him look older. Doesn't have a lot to say for himself. He bought a table from me about a year ago. Paid the asking price. Didn't make any attempt to beat me down — which makes a nice change, I must say."

"He bought a table from you?" It was still Bellamy asking the questions. Bert was happy to let him get on with it.

"Yes, I'm an antique dealer. Well — that's what the wife calls me. Second-hand furniture and bric-a-brac, you know the sort of thing! I've got two shops. One in Weybridge and another in Addlestone." He stood up. "Which reminds me, I should be in one of them right now."

"Yes, well — we won't detain you any longer, sir." Bert stood up to let him pass. The other police officers shuffled sideways out of the seats. "And we're very grateful to you for coming here. Now, this is what we'd like you to do during the next few days, Mr Corby. First of all, neither you nor your wife must mention this film to anyone — you understand? Secondly, keep well away from the camera shop and don't under any circumstances contact Mr Naylor."

"But supposing he contacts me? Supposing he finds out he's made a mistake and wants his film back?"

"In that case tell him you've been too busy to even look

61

at the film but you'll drop it in on him. Then do precisely nothing."

"Okay." Corby, gripping his valise with one hand, buttoned his raincoat with the other. "If that's what you want."

"That's what we want, Mr Corby."

"And what about my own film?"

"You'll get that back in due course, I promise you." Bert shook his hand. Corby turned to shake hands with Sam and Bellamy but they were keeping their distance. "And thank you again, sir. Hunter, will you take Mr Corby down to the front hall?"

When Corby and his escort had gone out Bert went to the door and closed it.

"Well, that's one for the book! I don't know who took that film and I don't know why. But one thing I do know. That girl could really put us in the picture — if only she'd talk. Check on this fellow Naylor, Bellamy, then get through to Hammersmith. Tell them to contact Brewster Bros. I want Jill Foster in your office by four o'clock this afternoon."

4

Surrey Snapshots was a small shop in a Shepperton side street. It had an attractive bow-fronted window which was stocked with an overcrowded display of cameras and photographers' equipment. A notice fixed to the inside of the glass claimed that Surrey Snapshots offered the fastest D & P service in the area. A narrow entry just wide enough for a car led through to the rear entrance of the premises. There was a flat over the shop, its front windows veiled by net curtains.

A few minutes after the sign hanging inside the semi-glazed door had been changed from "CLOSED 1–2 pm" to "OPEN" an inconspicuous dark blue Vauxhall drew up at the kerb twenty yards down the street. Two men got out and walked back towards the shop.

Bellamy had put on a hat to cover the patch on his head. As he led the way with his long stride Hunter followed at his own pace. A bell pinged as the Superintendent pushed the door open. The man behind the counter did not bother to look up. He was concentrating on the pieces of a faulty camera which he had taken apart on the shop counter. Bellamy recognised him from Corby's description. He had a sandy moustache, carefully trimmed so that it curved downwards on either side of his mouth. Behind him a curtain concealed the work-room at the rear.

Hunter had followed Bellamy in and closed the door before the shopkeeper deigned to glance up.

"Mr Naylor?" Bellamy's tone was stern, calculated to instil awe and respect into the shopkeeper. He failed to do so.

"Yes?"

"I'm Detective Superintendent Bellamy and this is Detective Sergeant Hunter. We're from Scotland Yard."

"I'm Arthur Naylor," Naylor responded, unimpressed. "From Shepperton. What can I do for you?"

"I understand a customer of yours — a Mr Leo Corby — called here yesterday morning and collected a film from you."

"That's quite right, he did." Naylor caught the eye of Hunter, who was quietly checking over the items in the shop. The Detective Sergeant's face remained dead-pan.

"The film was a 16mm cine film, in colour."

"Correct."

"We'd like you to tell us everything you know about that film, Mr Naylor."

"Everything I know?" Naylor put the pieces of the camera to one side. "Well — that won't be difficult. I don't know anything about it. Except that Mr Corby brought it here to be developed and I sent it off."

"Where did you send it?" Bellamy snapped. Leaning his stomach against the counter he was towering over the shopkeeper.

"To the Lab at Hemel Hempstead."

"When?"

"When?" Naylor's resentment at Bellamy's tone showed.

"Yes, when did you send the film to Hemel Hempstead?"

Naylor hesitated. Then he reached for a ledger that was lying open on the shelf behind him. He flipped a page back and ran his finger down a column before turning to Bellamy again.

"It went off a week today."

"And it was returned, when?"

"The day before yesterday." Naylor looked angrily at

Hunter, who had his back turned and was examining the window display from inside. "What's all this about?"

"How many films did you send to Hemel Hempstead on that particular day?"

"You mean — cine films?"

"Yes."

"Mr Corby's was the only one."

"Are you sure of that?"

"I'm absolutely sure. There hasn't been much cine work recently. Don't know why. Too expensive, I suppose."

"So when the Lab returned a cine film you took it for granted it was Mr Corby's?"

"Of course." Naylor's take-it-or-leave-it attitude abruptly changed. He glanced from Bellamy to Hunter and back again. "Wasn't it his film?"

"No, I'm afraid it wasn't. The Lab made a mistake and sent you the wrong film."

"You mean — the film I gave to Mr Corby wasn't his?"

"That's what I'm saying."

Naylor appeared absolutely nonplussed. His cockiness had vanished.

"Well, I'm sorry about this. Very sorry. Never known that to happen before. I only sent the one film so naturally I — " He pointed a finger at Bellamy. "Wait a minute! Did Mr Corby report this matter to the police?"

"Yes."

"Good heavens above!" Naylor exclaimed, his voice going up half an octave. "Why on earth do that? Why didn't he just return the film to me and ask me to get in touch with the Lab?"

"He had a reason," Bellamy said, gratified that he had brought the man to heel. He nodded towards the dismantled camera. "I can see you've got a problem on your hands so we won't take up any more of your time, sir."

Naylor's mouth was still hanging open as Bellamy turned towards the door. The bell pinged again. Hunter gave him an amused nod and followed the superintendent. When the door had closed Naylor moved out from behind the counter. He stood watching through the window as they climbed into the CID car and drove away. Then he locked the door and reversed the sign. As he went back to the counter the curtain over the opening parted. A small, plump man with a balding head came out. His chubby cheeks were creased by a smile.

"You did well, my friend," he said. "Full marks."

"What happens if they come back?"

"You play it cool and use your imagination." Corby reached into his hip pocket and pulled out a roll of twenty-pound notes. "Five hundred we said?"

The telephone box was in the corner of a quiet square not far from South Kensington underground station. Larry Voss had picked up the instrument and was dialling a number. He had no coins ready to insert if the call was answered. His companion was standing with his back propping the door open. Phil Morgan was a smaller, more stocky man with a black beard. He was wearing a short leather jacket, the kind favoured by motor-cyclists, and a pair of light, flared jeans. As he waited for Voss to make his call he idly watched the mid-afternoon Concorde making its approach run to London Airport. Though he admired its sleek shape he felt no yearnings to be in the pilot's seat. Like Voss, Morgan was a helicopter man.

Voss made seven circular movements with his finger then looked at the roof of the box, listening as the number began to ring. Morgan threw down his finished cigarette and put his foot on it.

"No answer, Larry?" Larry Voss gave the thumbs up sign. "He's out?"

"Yes."

Morgan squeezed into the box. Voss handed him the receiver.

"You know what to do?" Voss said. "If anyone answers, ring off. Otherwise stay with it."

Morgan nodded, put the receiver to his ear. "How long will it take you?"

"Not more than five minutes."

"Remember what I told you. Don't turn the place upside down — "

The door swung shut as Voss hurried away down the street. Morgan braced his feet against the side of the box and leant back. With one hand he fished out a packet of cigarettes and shook one out. The number continued to ring.

It took Voss three minutes to reach the converted Victorian house. He was carrying an envelope on which Sam Harvey's name and address was typed, with the words SPECIAL DELIVERY. Inside was a blank sheet of paper.

There was no one about as he climbed the stairs to the first floor. Outside Sam's door he paused. He could hear the continuous ringing of the telephone inside the flat. He took two keys from his pocket, pushed the longer one into the mortice lock and turned it. Then he inserted the Yale key and twisted it. The door yielded to his pressure. He went inside, securing both locks after him.

He folded the bogus envelope and put it in his pocket, then went into the sitting-room. He stood for a moment listening and looking. Mrs Carr had been that day. The flat was still tidy. The furniture was better quality than you would have expected in the home of a bachelor police officer.

He went to the desk and took out his handkerchief. He used it to lift the receiver. During the split second before the pay-tone began to bleep he quickly said: "I'm in." Then he heard the dialling tone and knew that Phil Morgan had hung up.

Jill Foster was tense and nervy as she came out through the glass door of Brewster Bros. As she hurried towards the Ford Granada Ghia parked on the forecourt she kept breaking into a half-run every few paces. A rasping roar drew her attention to the sky. Like thousands of other Londoners she looked skywards and recognised the unmistakeable silhouette of Concorde.

She opened the unlocked door and slipped into the driver's seat. As if the car were a sanctuary to which she had been fleeing she lowered her head and covered her face with her hands. The sound of Concorde, echoing from the walls of buildings, gradually faded. With an effort she sat up, groped in her handbag and inserted the ignition key in its slot. The engine started smoothly. She was about to drive away when she saw a police car come down the street from the direction of Hammersmith Broadway. It braked and swung into the forecourt of Brewster Bros. She quickly bent forward over the telephone set between the two front seats. She heard the doors of the police car bang and prayed that they had not seen her. Her heart was beating fast. When she dared to raise her head the police car was parked opposite the glass doors, but the policemen had vanished.

She engaged gear, drove quickly out into the street, cutting across the bows of a delivery van.

*   *   *

Peter Brewster was in his office talking to his white-coated foreman and one of the mechanics when the two police officers came in. Apparently unconcerned he waved them towards the space furnished with tables and chairs where customers for the car-hire service filled in their forms. The policemen accepted the hint but they did not sit down. Brewster took his time about finishing his conversation with his employees, then sauntered over towards his visitors.

The smaller, younger one was in plain clothes. His companion was a beefy constable in uniform with a flat, peaked cap.

"Sorry about that. What can I do for you, gentlemen?"

"I'm Detective Sergeant Halford, sir," the plain-clothes man said. "I understand that you have a Miss Foster, Miss Jill Foster, in your employ?"

"That's correct. She's one of our drivers. But you people are well aware of that. You've been here before."

Halford ignored the comment. "We'd very much like to have a word with Miss Foster, if that's possible."

"I'm afraid it's not possible. Not at the moment. She's out on a job."

"When will she be back, sir?"

"Difficult to say." Brewster consulted the large electric clock on his wall. "I would guess about — six o'clock. Perhaps even later. She's in Brighton at the moment. Is there anything I can do, Sergeant?"

"No, I don't think there is. Thank you, sir." Halford looked thoughtfully at Brewster's innocently helpful face. "Oh, perhaps you could verify Miss Foster's address." He took out his notebook and flipped the pages over. "28A Ladbroke Grove, W10."

"I think that's correct. I'll check it for you. I believe she moved about two months ago — " Brewster moved round behind his desk. He tried every drawer before he found the right one and even then he had difficulty in identifying his address book. "Ah, here we are! Yes, you're perfectly right. 28A Ladbroke Grove."

"Thank you, sir," Halford said with sarcastic emphasis.

Jill turned left onto Hammersmith Broadway. Traffic was heavy as she threaded her way past Olympia and on into Kensington High Street. She was an expert, decisive driver. She could jink the big Ford past lumbering buses and heavy vehicles as if it was a Mini. Using side streets like a taxi driver she threaded her way through to Lillee Road. As she waited there for the lights to change the telephone beside her seat rang.

As she had expected the caller was Peter Brewster.

"Are you all right?"

"Yes," she said doubtfully.

"You only just made it."

"I know. I saw them."

"Not to worry," he said with maddening cheerfulness.

"I am worried, Peter. Desperately worried."

"I've told you. I'll take care of everything. There's really nothing for you to worry about."

Ahead of her the lights had turned green.

"Do you mean that, Peter?"

"Yes, I do. See you tonight. Eight o'clock."

"I'll be there."

"It won't be like last time, I hope?"

"No," she said. Some colour had come back into her face and she was smiling now. "It won't be like last time."

"You've got the address?"

"Yes. You've given it to me often enough."

"Well — take care. And don't do anything stupid."

The car in front was already moving and the taxi behind

her had started hooting. She put the receiver down quickly. The Granada moved forward with a jerk. Despite Brewster's reassurances she was still edgy enough to be rattled by a bullying taxi driver.

He was still on her tail when she was checked by lights a quarter of a mile from South Kensington underground station. He drew up level with her on the inside. She did not deign to look in his direction, though she was aware that something odd was happening. His fare had decided to get out and was standing between the taxi and the Ford, thrusting notes at the driver. Jill had her eyes on the lights and it was only when the passenger door of her own car was opened that her head jerked round.

To her astonishment a man was getting in beside her. She recognised him as the tall, good-looking one she had last seen in the Italian restaurant.

"What do you think you're doing?" she jerked out, both angry and frightened.

"This must be my lucky day!" Sam said, grinning. He slammed the door. "You're just the person I want to see."

"Get out of this car!"

"Better move on. You're holding up the traffic."

"You heard what I said." Jill's face was white. "Get out of this car!"

"And you heard what I said," Sam answered, unruffled. "Get moving."

"If you don't get out of this car — " Jill reached forward as if to switch the ignition off and remove the key. Behind the Granada impatient drivers had the palms of their hands on their horns.

"Do you want to cause an accident?" Suddenly Sam's tone was that of a police officer. "Now, just do as I say. Drive on. I'll tell you where to go."

She glared at him, but when she saw that the smile had gone she changed her mind. Her hand dropped to the gear lever.

"Now, perhaps you'll tell me what this is all about and let me go. I have an appointment at five o'clock."

Sam closed the door of his flat and followed her in. She was still keeping up her act of outraged innocence but he knew that it was a cover for her nervousness.

"It's all about you, Miss Foster." Sam took his coat off and flung it over a chair. She was facing him with assumed defiance, her back to the window-embrasure. "Now, listen to me. You don't deserve this but I'm going to give you a choice."

"What do you mean? A choice of what?"

"We can go to Scotland Yard where you will be interrogated by a very tough former colleague of mine called Superintendent Bellamy or you can tell me the whole story. I'll give you just twenty seconds to make up your mind."

Behind Jill the long curtains billowed out a little as if stirred by a draught. But the sun was in Sam's eyes and in any case he was concentrating too hard on Jill to notice that the windows were shut.

"What story? I don't know what you're talking about."

"I think you do. Now, which is it to be?"

"What is it you want to know?"

"I want to know exactly what happened after you picked my parents up at the airport."

"I didn't pick them up. I *took* them to the airport. You know that. You were with me."

"That was in the morning. At about eleven o'clock. Some hours later — I don't know exactly what time it was, but early in the afternoon — you returned and picked them up again."

She had been holding her breath. Now she let it out in a gasp. "I don't know what you're talking about."

"I think you do. Where did you take my parents?"

"I tell you I didn't take them anywhere! I had other jobs to do. I had to pick up a party from the Dorchester Hotel—"

"Miss Foster," Sam interrupted quietly. "You are not telling the truth. You are lying—"

"How dare you—"

"I saw you pick them up that afternoon."

Her mouth fell open. She unconsciously backed away a step and came up against the desk.

"You were wearing a light blue Burberry with a scarf to match. The car you were driving bore the registration number HNO 967—"

"How could you have seen me? You were back at your—"

She stopped and bit her lip. He knew now that she was going to give way.

"It's not quite literally true that I saw you with my own eyes. But I saw a film. A colour film, obviously taken by an amateur. It showed my parents coming out of Terminal 3 and crossing the roadway. Then a Jaguar drove up and you got out. My father put his luggage in the boot and then got into the back of the car with my mother. Then you drove away towards the tunnel that leads out of the airport."

Jill was shaking her head from side to side. The strength had gone out of her legs and she was leaning for support against the edge of the desk.

"Are you telling me the truth?" she said, almost inaudibly.

"Yes, I am."

"Then — who took this film?"

"I don't know who took it."

"But — you've seen it?"

"Yes."

"Where did you see it?" she said desperately. "Where did you see this film?"

"At Scotland Yard. It was delivered to a colleague of mine, Chief Superintendent Sinclair."

She was staring at him, wide-eyed. Then she broke, turning away from him and burying her face in her hands.

"Oh, my God!"

Sam did not move. He had seen women put on acts like this before.

"I've answered your questions. Now please answer mine. Where did you take my mother and father?"

"I — I can't tell you." She shook her head, still hiding her face. "I daren't tell you."

"You've got to tell me. If you don't, believe me, you'll be in real trouble."

"I'm in trouble now," she said, in little more than a whisper.

"Where did you take them?" Sam demanded, his voice hard.

"I took them to a house outside of London."

"Where, outside London?"

"I'm sorry, I — I don't remember where."

"Why did you take them there?"

"I was told to. I had — instructions."

"From whom?"

"A man telephoned me. He said I had to take them to that particular house because that's where the van was."

"The van with Marius of Rye on it?"

"Yes."

"Who was this man?"

"I'm sorry, I can't tell you. I've said too much already."

She straightened up and turned her back on him. Sam was subconsciously rubbing the smooth indent on the second finger of his right hand. He was not a bully by nature and he was coming to believe that her distress was genuine.

"You said just now that you were in trouble."

"I am in trouble," she said, voice very low. "Deep trouble."

"Then listen to me." He moved closer and took her arm. "If you're prepared to tell me who this man was and where exactly you took my parents — I'll do everything in my power to help you."

She turned back towards him.

"I don't think anyone can help me. Not now. It's too late."

"I wouldn't be too sure about that, if I were you." She seemed reassured by his changed tone and attitude. "Look — I think the best thing we can both do right now is have a drink. Then we'll talk. What do you say to that?"

She nodded and allowed herself to be steered towards the settee.

"You sit down there, Jill. I'll fix a couple of drinks. I think something strong is called for. Do you like ice with your whisky?"

"No ice. Do you have any soda water?"

"I think so."

She nodded again and sat down. As he went towards the kitchen she was reaching for her bag, already thinking about her appearance.

Sam went into the kitchen, shaking his head. He would never understand the vagaries of women. A minute ago she had been on the verge of hysteria and here she was worrying about her make up and requesting soda water with her whisky.

He looked in the fridge. No soda water. He opened the door of the larder and squatted down to peer into the lower shelf. The door, as always, swung shut and banged him on the backside, making the place darker than before.

He was cursing it when from the sitting-room came a terrified scream, then a shout which sounded like: "No, Voss, no! Please — don't".

Then there was silence.

Sam straightened up. His head banged the storage fixture on the inside of the door. Potatoes, onions and a cucumber rained down on him. He slammed the offending door back, skidded round the kitchen table and lunged into the sitting-room.

From the direction of the hall came the sound of the front door being slammed. He started in pursuit but as he came round the end of the sofa he almost fell over Jill Foster. She was lying on her side. Blood was pouring from one temple and the handle of a knife protruded from her back.

The only magazine of interest in the waiting-room of the hospital was a copy of Thoroughbred and Classic Cars. Sam had already perused it while waiting for the verdict on Bellamy. Now he had it in his hands again. This time he was scanning the advertisement columns of second-hand cars to see whether his 911E had appreciated in value. After an hour he threw it down on the table. He stared gloomily at a sign which read IF YOU MUST SMOKE PLEASE DO SO IN THE OUTER HALL.

A nurse whom he had seen escorting Jill's stretcher to the operating theatre came bustling down the corridor. By moving fast he was just able to intercept her as she passed the open entrance to the waiting area.

"Nurse! Can you please tell me what's happening?"

She switched her thoughts from the patient in Ward 4,

made her voice calm as she answered. "You haven't seen the doctor?"

"No. I haven't."

"You haven't seen Dr Majduli?"

"I told you I hadn't. I haven't seen anyone and I've been here over an hour."

She glanced over her shoulder. A young Indian doctor in a white coat was coming down the corridor. In a dark face the heavy shadows round his eyes were like charcoal. The nurse went to meet him and said a few words in a low voice. The doctor's eyes focussed on Sam. He nodded and came towards him.

"I'm Dr Majduli. You wish to see me?"

His English was good with only a trace of accent.

"Yes. I want to know how Miss Foster is."

The nurse, obviously worried, interposed: "Sister in Ward 4 would like to see you as soon as possible, Doctor."

"I'm sure she would, Nurse, and I'll be there as soon as possible, but I haven't yet discovered how to be in two places at once. Not yet. But not to worry, I'm working on it."

The nurse pursed her lips and hurried on her way. Dr Majduli looked at Sam, waiting.

"How is Miss Foster?" Sam asked again.

"Are you a relative, Mr — ?"

"No, I'm Superintendent Harvey, Scotland Yard."

"Oh, I'm sorry! I didn't realise you were the police. The nurse never told me. She's going to be all right, Superintendent. There's very little internal bleeding and we've sewn up the tissues and closed the wound up with half a dozen stitches. She'll be okay, I'm sure."

"Could I have a word with her?"

"I'd rather you didn't. She's only just coming out of the anaesthetic. Tomorrow morning perhaps, but not tonight, if you don't mind. You wouldn't get much sense out of her anyway."

"Will you be on duty tomorrow morning, Doctor?"

"Will I be — " Dr Majduli's professional manner cracked. Gleaming white teeth showed as the dark face was lit by a smile. "You must be joking! I'm always on duty." With a cheerful wave he turned to go to Ward 4. "See you tomorrow."

Darkness had fallen by the time Sam returned to his flat. Following the ambulancemen out he'd been careful to lock the door properly, though by now he was sure someone had a set of keys to the place. His home was becoming very accident-prone. Twice in three days he had needed to dial 999 and call the ambulance.

He was reasonably sure as he came in, switching on lights, that no one had visited his flat since he had left in such a hurry. He took his coat off and threw it over the back of the chair, then went into the kitchen. The bottle of whisky was still standing beside the sink, with the stopper out. He poured a large measure into one of the two glasses he had put out, added a little water from the tap. As he walked back to the sitting-room, brow wrinkled in thought, the lights from the square shone at him through the uncurtained window. He crossed to draw the curtains. As he did so he saw a mark on the carpet close to the wainscot at the side of the window. He stooped down and touched it with his finger. Damp mud from someone's heel. Workmen had taken up the pavement a little way down the square to repair a gas leak.

He straightened up and switched on the standard lamp by the end of the settee. Its light fell on the small patch of blood on the carpet where Jill had lain, half on her right side. He saw now what had escaped him in his anxiety to save her life — her handbag, lying half hidden under the settee.

He picked it up, cleared the low table of books and magazines and laid the contents of the handbag out on it. There were the usual items — a wallet with notes and a bank card, a comb in a leather case, several keys on a ring, a packet of cigarettes, a gold lighter, a pen and a book of matches. The lipstick had fallen off her lap as she had stood up to face her attacker.

He began to replace the articles, examining each one carefully as he did so. He left the book-matches till last. Why did she need book-matches when she had a gold lighter? They had obviously been given away free by the establishment advertised on the front flap — "THE PRINCE HAL. Your friendly pub." He flipped the flap back. All the matches had been removed. The blank inside had been used as a miniature note or memo pad.

MR HOGARTH?
01.876 0295
748 2269
935 8692

Sam reached for the packet of cigarettes he had removed from the coffee table. Still looking at the name and the three telephone numbers, he used Jill's lighter on his own cigarette. He sat down on the sofa and leant back.

By the time he had finished his cigarette he had made up his mind. He stubbed it out, went across to his desk and pulled the telephone towards him. He did not need to refer again to the book-matches before dialling the first number.

Sam had taken part in amateur dramatics at school and prided himself on his Cockney accent. Like every good actor he had adopted the posture and facial expression of the character he was playing before the call was answered.

"Yes," snapped an uncompromising voice.

"What number are you?" Along with the Cockney accent Sam had lowered his voice and made it rougher.

"What number do you want?"

"Are you 876 0295?"

"Who is that calling?"

"This is the engineer, sir. Your number's been reported out of order — "

"There's nothing wrong with this number. You got through all right, didn't you?"

"Must be some mistake, sir. What's the name of the subscriber?"

"I'm the subscriber," the voice said. "Walter Randell."

And Walter Randell slammed down the receiver.

The second number struck a chord in Sam's mind.

This time there was a longer delay before he was answered.

"748 2269."

The voice was crisp and impatient. It sounded ominously familiar.

" 'Oos that speakin'?"

"Bellamy speaking. Who is this, please?"

Sam quickly adjusted his posture and facial expression.

"Ah — Superintendent Bellamy?"

"Is that you, Harvey? Your voice sounds funny."

Bellamy was out of breath. Sam knew he was a keep-fit maniac. He'd probably been out jogging or doing a ton-up on his stationary bicycle.

"I've got a bit of a cold."

"What is it you want? If it's not urgent, let me ring you back."

"I — ah — just wondered how you made out at the camera shop."

"According to Naylor the lab made a mistake but I'm not too sure about our Mr Naylor — I don't quite know why. Look — do you mind? Can I ring you back on this some other time?"

"Don't worry. That's all I wanted to know."

"I've sent Sinclair a memo. He knows all about it."

Feeling a little foolish Sam rang off. He reached for the book-matches and repeated the third number to himself a few times. He was certain he had never used it before.

The answering voice was again a man's, but this time coarse and uneducated.

"This is the Telephone Engineer, sir." Sam went into his act again. "I understand you're 'avin' trouble. What exactly happens to be the matter with your phone?"

"There's nothing the matter with it, mate, so far as I know."

"It's been reported, sir," Sam reproved him.

"Not by me, it hasn't."

"You are 935 8692?" Sam said in the tone of petty officialdom.

"That's right."

"Are you the subscriber?"

"I pay the bills, if that's what you mean."

"Your address is 28 King Edward Mansions? Name of White?"

"You're on the wrong wavelength, mate. This is 33 Galloway Street. Name of Voss."

"Sorry, sir. I was lookin' at the wrong sheet. Must be some mistake. Sorry you've been troubled."

"No trouble, mate. Any time — "

Sam put the receiver down. He went into his bedroom, took off his jacket and put on a loose-fitting anorak. Pushing his wallet into the inside pocket he moved to the kitchen. The dishwashing machine was under one side of the sink. When the door was opened it revealed not the

81

usual wire racks but a second door. Sam used two keys to open the door of this concealed safe, which had escaped the notice of whoever had searched his flat. He reached inside and withdrew a police revolver. He confirmed what he knew already, that there were six rounds in the chambers. He relocked the safe, straightened up and pushed the gun into the pocket of the anorak.

Galloway Street was in Pimlico. As he turned into it Sam noticed the telephone box on the corner. The street-lighting was dim. There was no traffic and only a few pedestrians. He cruised slowly between the lines of parked cars, checking up on the house numbers. He realised he'd passed number 33 when he saw a white 57 on a gate. He put the Porsche in the next parking space, replaced the ABC street guide in the glove compartment and locked the car carefully before starting to walk back up the pavement.

No 33 was a rather delapidated house converted to flats about ten years ago. With the rise in crime an outer door with an entry phone had been fitted more recently. Sam had to use his torch to read the names. Flat 4 was occupied by L. Voss.

Sam pressed the button on the same line.

"Who is it?"

Voss's voice sounded even coarser, distorted by the speaker.

"Mr Voss?"

"Yes."

"Telephone Engineer, sir. Sorry to trouble you again, but we've had complaints from callers gettin' no ringin' tone on your number. I'd like to check your installation. It'll only take a few minutes. If it's inconvenient we can call back tomorrow."

"Come along up," Voss said. "It's on the second floor."

There was the sound of a buzzer. The lock on the door clicked and it sprang open two inches. Sam pushed it wide and walked in. There was no lift. Someone had parked a bicycle at the bottom of the stairs, chaining it to the banisters. Sam climbed to the second floor. There was only one door. The number 4 was slightly askew on it. It was ajar. With his right hand in his anorak pocket, he used his left to knock.

"Come in," Voss called from inside the flat.

Sam prodded the door with his foot. It swung back revealing a narrow hallway. As he entered he used his foot again to close it. The door at the end was open. He could see tables and chairs. He walked slowly to the entrance of the lounge. On the threshold he stopped. Larry Voss was sitting in an armchair facing the doorway. He was about five paces away. He was holding an automatic pistol in his hand and there was a welcoming smile on his face. The automatic was pointing at Sam's stomach.

"Come in, Harvey. I've been expecting you."

"Yes," Sam said, eyeing the gun. "I rather gather that."

"Get your hands out of your pockets where I can see them."

Sam did as he was told.

The furniture in the room was clumsily arranged. There were several ghastly prints on the walls and a rather attractive Victorian mirror above the fireplace. A small suitcase stood on the floor beside Voss's chair.

"Sit down, I want to talk to you."

Sam stood where he was. "I want to talk to you too, Mr Voss. That's why I'm here. Unless I'm very much mistaken you've searched my flat, on more than one occasion. Why?"

"Can't you guess why?"

"I can only assume that you were looking for something. I can't imagine what it was."

"I must confess I find that difficult to believe. But since I failed to find what I was after, I'll give you the benefit of the doubt. However, we'll talk about that later. Right now, I want to hear about Jill Foster. I want to know what happened when you picked her up."

"You know what happened, you bastard!" Sam said equably. "We went back to my place. You were there. You stuck a knife into the poor girl."

"What happened before then — in the car?"

"Nothing *happened*."

Voss pushed the automatic forward threateningly.

"What did you talk about? What did she tell you?"

"Well, if you must know," Sam said, casually, "we talked about the firm she worked for, Brewster Bros, most of the time. Oh, and come to think about it, I believe she made an oblique reference to someone called Bellamy. The only Bellamy I could think of was Superintendent Bellamy. 'Memo' Bellamy, his colleagues call him. But I doubt very much whether she was referring to him."

"I don't believe a bloody word you've said!"

Sam shrugged. "Mr Voss, it's a matter of complete indifference to me whether you believe me or not."

Voss stood up. If he was trying to look dangerous he succeeded.

"It'll be interesting to see how long your indifference lasts, Harvey. Put your hands above your head and turn round."

Sam hoped that Voss was about to offer him the chance he needed, but he did not want to appear too eager to obey the command. The gun was steady. The distance between them was about ten feet. To reach for his own weapon would be fatal.

"You think I'd be such a fool as to turn my back on you?"

"You'd be more of a fool not to. Don't think I wouldn't use this thing. Now, put your hands up and turn round!"

Sam stared into the close-set eyes, then he put his hands above his head and slowly turned round. Voss moved quickly up behind him. The barrel of the automatic was pushed against his back. He felt Voss's left hand feeling for the gun in his anorak pocket. The adrenalin was pumping through his body, his muscles flexed.

Suddenly he twisted to his right and flailed downwards with his right arm. As his body turned at right angles to the gun the edge of his open hand struck Voss on the wrist. Voss's trigger finger tightened a split second too late. The detonation in that confined space was deafening. The bullet ripped through Sam's anorak and embedded itself in the wall. The gun dropped from Voss's hand. Sam, facing him now, kicked it out of reach, but he was surprised by the swiftness of the other man's reflexes. As he straightened up Voss drove his fist into Sam's groin. The pain was agonising. Involuntarily Sam doubled up, a bloodshot blackness before his eyes.

Voss clutched his right wrist. He stared wild-eyed from the gun to the reeling superintendent. He did not notice the hole in the wall. Then he panicked. He rushed headlong into the hall and out of the flat. Sam, in a daze, heard his footsteps pounding down the stairs three at a time.

He recovered his vision quickly. The pain from his groin was spreading in waves through the lower part of his body. Still half doubled he staggered out to the front door. Below him at street level he heard the outer door close on its spring. He shut the door of the flat and pushed up the knob which secured the Yale lock.

Back in the sitting-room he picked up the glass from which Voss had been drinking. Whisky, and nearly neat too. He knocked it back and began to feel better.

Before searching the room he decided to investigate the suitcase. It was locked. There was no sign of keys. He retrieved Voss's automatic. The shot must have been audible to anyone else in the building. Unless they were very foolish they would not come knocking at the door. Most likely they had already telephoned the police. A patrol car could be here within minutes.

He shielded his face with his arm and used the automatic as a key. Two shots disposed of the two locks. He dumped the contents on the floor and quickly searched through them. There seemed to be nothing except clothes and personal effects of Mr Larry Voss. He picked up the suitcase again and examined the interior. He took out his key ring and used the small knife on it to rip out the lining of the base. Concealed beneath it were two post-card sized photographs.

The first photograph was of Jason Harvey's Austin Maxi parked on a country road. Jason was about to enter the driver's seat. It was obvious that he was unaware that someone was taking his picture — probably with a telescopic lens.

The second was more puzzling still. It showed a very attractive yacht at anchor in a harbour. Sam thought he recognised Poole Harbour in Dorset. The name on the bow of the yacht was just legible. "Easy Living."

The sound of a police two-tone horn was echoing in a street not far away. Sam straightened up. His discovery had been a good cure for pain. He put the two photographs in the breast pocket of his anorak, zipped it up as he headed for the front door.

As he came out of the house and turned left to walk towards his own car a police patrol car stormed into Galloway Street, its blue light flashing.

To Sam's surprise it did not stop at number 33 but raced

past him towards the corner where he had noticed the telephone box. He saw now that a crowd had collected. An ambulance was just arriving from the opposite direction to the police car.

Sam turned and walked back. By the time he got to the street corner a body on a stretcher was being loaded into the ambulance. The police were trying to persuade the bystanders to move on. Among them was a young woman with striking blonde hair. She was wearing a light brown leather coat, expensive shoes and a Hermes scarf. Sam was surprised to see such a well-dressed woman, but he had learnt that the most unexpected people take a ghoulish interest in accidents.

"What happened?" he asked a man who was standing on the fringe of the crowd.

"Someone knocked down by a car, I think. Another bloody hit-and-run motorist."

As the ambulance doors were closed Sam turned away and started to walk back towards his car.

He had slid into the seat and was fastening his seat-belt when a Mini Metro pulled up. It stopped so that the driver's window was exactly opposite Sam's window. He glanced round and saw that the driver was the woman in the brown leather coat. She was winding her window down, signalling that she wanted to talk to him.

Sam quickly checked to see if there was anyone else near his car before he lowered his own window.

"I thought you might like to know," she said. "It wasn't an accident."

Sam did not show his surprise. "What did happen?"

She was watching his reaction with interest, a faint smile on her face.

"About ten minutes ago a shot was fired inside number 33. Almost immediately a man came rushing out through the front door. He was in a state of panic. He looked to right and left, then started running down the street. When he reached the telephone box he blundered inside and started desperately searching his pocket for coins."

Sam was listening in amazement. Why had she stopped to give him this blow-by-blow account?

"He found coins in the end, and dialled the number. He was talking for perhaps three minutes. As he stepped onto the pavement a car turned into the street. Its headlights lit the man up. He turned and seemed to know what was going to happen. He backed away towards the wall, shielding his face with his arms. I think he expected shots. But the car veered towards him, mounted the pavement and crushed him against the wall. Then it reversed and drove away. The man's name was Larry Voss."

As she began to wind her window up Sam shouted: "Who are you? How do you know all this?"

She only smiled back, then put her foot on the accelerator. By the time he had turned the Porsche in the narrow street the Metro had vanished.

5

Bert Sinclair arrived on Sam's doorstep even before Mrs Carr had turned up. He was in a very bad mood and was brandishing a copy of *The Daily World*. Without waiting to be invited he strode into the sitting-room. As usual at this time of the morning it was littered with the remains of Sam's breakfast, which he'd consumed as he prowled about the room.

"Have you seen this?" the Chief Superintendent demanded.

He thrust the folded newspaper under Sam's nose.

'MARIUS OF RYE' MYSTERY DEEPENS

by Chris Morris

Jill Foster, the girl who drove Mr and Mrs Jason Harvey to the airport, was herself attacked last night after dining with Superintendent Harvey at a restaurant in Kensington —

The article was illustrated by three photographs, the familiar picture of the white van after the murders, an attractive head and shoulders shot of Jill Foster and a much less attractive photo of Sam Harvey coming out of Scotland Yard. This last had been taken some years ago.

"Yes, I've just been reading it."

"What the devil does it mean?" Bert said, shaking the paper. "Did you take that girl out to dinner last night?"

"No, I didn't."

"Well — what the hell is all this?"

"Bert, calm down! I've every intention of telling you what happened."

"Sam, you owe me an explanation." The Chief Superintendent wagged a finger threateningly, "And by God it had better be good!"

"All right, Bert," Sam said placatingly. "After our meeting at the Yard I thought it might help if I had another talk with Jill Foster."

"So you knew damn well we were going to pick her up! You shouldn't have interfered, Sam."

"What do you mean — interfered?"

Bert saw that Sam was not in a mood to be needled. He made an effort to moderate his tone. "Sam, I know how desperately worried you've been. But you've got to realise that Bellamy is investigating this case, not you."

"In other words, keep my nose out of things?"

"That's about it, Sam." Bert threw the paper onto the settee and sat in one of the chairs. "Now tell me what happened yesterday."

"I was in a taxi on my way to Brewster Bros when, purely by chance, I saw Jill Foster. I jumped out of the taxi and — well, to cut the story short I persuaded her to come back here. She was nervous and very much on edge so, in an attempt to put her at her ease, I offered her a drink. Whilst I was in the kitchen a man called Larry Voss came out from behind that curtain. The bastard attacked her with a knife."

"Larry Voss?"

"Yes."

As he listened Bert's anger had given way to intense interest.

"A man called Voss was murdered last night, in Pimlico."

"Yes, I know. It was the same man."

90

Bert was studying Sam shrewdly as he asked: "Were you in Pimlico last night?"

"Yes, I was." Sam gave his half smile. "And now you're going to ask me what I was doing there and I'm not going to tell you. But I promise you, if I discover anything of importance — of real importance — I'll put you in the picture."

"The operative words being 'of real importance', I suppose?" Bert gave the younger man a wry look. "All right, Sam. Do things your way. You've always been a loner, ever since I've known you. But that's off the record — and just you remember that! Now tell me about this fellow Morris."

"Morris?"

"The chap who wrote this article." Bert reached across for the paper and tapped it with the back of his hand. "Chris Morris. How did he get hold of this nonsense about the restaurant? I presume it is nonsense?"

"Yes, of course it is. He must have invented it."

Sam was drifting round the room, collecting the cup, saucer and plates and putting them back on his breakfast tray.

"Did he show up at the hospital?"

"Not to my knowledge. But I don't know him, so he could have done. He certainly didn't contact me."

The doorbell rang — two persistent peals.

"That could be Bellamy," Bert said. "I told him to meet me here. He's been to the hospital."

Sam took the tray into the kitchen before going to open the door. Bellamy was down on one knee, doing up his shoe-lace. He had removed the dressing from his scalp. There was still a bald spot with a crusty wound in the middle of it. He squinted up at Sam.

"Is Sinclair here?"

"Yes, come in." As Bellamy rose to his considerable height, Sam said. "Having trouble with your laces, Bellamy?"

"Yes, it broke."

"You should wear slip-ons."

"I don't like them," Bellamy grumbled, following Sam into the sitting-room. "I have a high instep."

"Hello, Bellamy." Bert waved a hand without getting up. "What's the news? How is she?"

"Miss Foster's only fair, I'm afraid," Bellamy told him gloomily.

"Did you see her?"

"Yes, with difficulty. The Doctor wasn't keen — "

"Wait a minute," Sam interjected. "What does that mean — she's only fair?"

"The doctor says she's still suffering from shock. Having talked to the girl — or tried to talk to her — I can understand what he means."

"What did she say?"

"Not a great deal." Bellamy shook his head. This morning his face was longer than ever. "She either doesn't remember what happened yesterday afternoon, or she's frightened and just won't talk."

"Bellamy," Sam insisted. "What *did* she say?"

Bellamy looked at Sam with an expression which implied: you asked for this. "She said that you picked her up and forced her to come back here with you. She said you questioned her and when she refused to answer your questions you offered her a drink."

"That's not strictly true," Sam commented mildly.

"It's true so far as I'm concerned," Bellamy said belligerently. "That's what she told me."

"What else did she tell you?" Bert prompted.

"Nothing else. That's all."

"Didn't you ask her what happened? Didn't you ask her who it was that — "

"Yes, of course I did, sir!" Bellamy looked injured. "She says she doesn't remember who attacked her. She doesn't remember anything about it."

"We know who attacked her," Sam told him. "It was a man called Voss."

"Voss?" echoed Bellamy, surprised. "Larry Voss?"

"Yes. Do you know him?"

"Yes. I know Voss. He's an ex-helicopter pilot. He was kicked out of the service for — " Bellamy's eyes moved from Sam to Bert. "If this is true, why haven't we picked him up?"

"He's dead," Bert said quietly. "He was murdered."

"Voss — murdered?"

"Yes, he was hit by a car. Last night. In Pimlico."

"I didn't know that." Bellamy took a turn round the settee, finally coming face to face with Sam. "How do you know that it was Voss who attacked Jill Foster? Did you see him?"

"No, but you can take my word for it. It was Voss."

"I'm not prepared to take your word for it, Harvey. I want the facts."

Sam stared back into his angry face. "The facts are that, unbeknown to me, Larry Voss was here, in the flat, when we arrived. I went into the kitchen to get some Scotch and while I was in there he attacked her."

"But you didn't see him?"

"I've already told you I didn't."

"Frankly, Harvey, I'm not at all happy about this."

Sam forced a smile. "That makes two of us."

Sam had done his best to clean up the bloodstain on his carpet but there was no concealing it from Mrs Carr. He had to invent a story about an accident with a pot of coffee. She shook her head very sceptically and he was far from sure she believed him. To keep her in a good mood he spent some time chatting her up before going out to the hall to put on his belted mackintosh. It was raining hard outside.

He was about to open the front door when his telephone rang. He hesitated, then decided to go back and answer it.

"Hello? Sam Harvey speaking."

"Mr Harvey, this is Margaret Randell."

"Oh — good morning, Margaret."

"I hope I'm not disturbing you."

"No, as a matter of fact you've just caught me. I was on my way out."

"I don't suppose you were coming down here, by any chance?"

"No, I wasn't. But I could come down if you particularly want to see me."

"Well — it's just that — " She hesitated, then seemed to make her mind up. Her voice became louder as if she'd cupped her hand round her mouth. "I've been reading about last night, about what happened to that girl."

Sam realised that this would not be a short conversation. By holding the telephone with his chin he'd managed to take off his raincoat. He tossed it over the back of the nearest chair.

"Jill Foster?"

"Yes. There's a picture of her in my paper and — well, I'm pretty sure she's the girl I told you about."

"You mean the girl you saw — with the boy?"

"Yes. I'm not a hundred per cent certain, but I *think* it's the same girl."

"Thank you for telling me, Margaret."

"I didn't know whether to mention it or not, but you did say if there was anything — "

"I'm glad you've telephoned because I wanted to talk to you anyway."

"Oh?" She sounded eager and a little flattered. "About what?"

"About your husband, or rather your ex-husband."

"Walter? What about him?" Her voice had changed, become harder. "Has he been troubling you again?"

"No, it's just that he made me curious, talking about you the way he did. And I wondered — "

"What is it you want to know about Walter?" Margaret asked, all the friendliness gone.

"What does he do exactly?"

"You mean — for a living?"

"Yes."

She laughed. "That's a very good question. And it's not the first time I've been asked it. He calls himself a Financial Consultant but — Well, not to put too fine a point on it, he's a gambler."

"You mean — a professional gambler?"

"That's right. Baccarat, roulette, poker, horses, dogs, the lot. You name it, he plays it."

"Well, I must say that surprises me. Appearances can be deceptive after all."

"They certainly can so far as Walter is concerned."

Sam could not help laughing at her caustic tone.

"Thank you for calling, Margaret. I shall probably pop down to Guildford in the next two or three days."

"I shall look forward to seeing you," Margaret said, the smile back in her voice. "Though you don't need to worry about Pennymore. I go in every day."

Sam's Porsche was parked in the space reserved for residents about fifty yards from his flat. He was hurrying towards it when a car pulled in to the kerb just ahead of him. He was level with it when the door opened.

"Mr Harvey!"

Sam checked and turned round.

"You remember me." A young man was getting out of the car. "Peter Brewster from Brewster Bros."

"Yes, I remember you. What can I do for you?"

Brewster slammed his door. "I'd appreciate it if you could — " He groped for words, evidently embarrassed. "I'd very much like to have a few words with you — if you can spare a few minutes."

"There's a coffee shop round the corner. Let's go and talk there."

Brewster nodded gratefully. He quickly grabbed an umbrella and locked the door of his car, then fell into step beside Sam.

Sam said, "I imagine you've seen the papers or rather *the* paper?"

"Yes, I have." Brewster put up his umbrella. "Mr Harvey, I don't know what happened last night, and it's none of my business — "

Sam gave him a direct look.

"If it's none of your business, why are you here?"

"I'm here because — Look, I don't know what Jill told you — about me, I mean."

"What makes you think she told me anything about you, Mr Brewster?"

"I'm quite sure she did, and I'd like you to hear my side of the story."

"All right. Go ahead."

"Jill's a damned attractive girl and for some time now I've been trying to — well, get to first base with her. I don't like to boast, but frankly, I don't usually have a problem when it comes to — "

"Forgive the interruption, Mr Brewster, but I'm old-fashioned. I like a story to have a beginning, a middle, and an end."

They came to the place where the pavement had been taken up. The workmen had gone off and left a gaping hole surrounded by a flimsy barrier. Brewster dropped back to let Sam circumvent it, then had to run to catch up.

"Okay, I'll start at the beginning. About a week ago I received an anonymous letter saying that Jill had not only forged her references but that she had, in fact, once been arrested for shoplifting. I questioned Jill about it and she admitted that it was true. I told her I didn't want to be difficult, after all she was good at her job, and providing we got along well together I could see no reason why — "

"You don't have to explain all this to me."

"Well — yesterday afternoon she came to see me. She told me that she was once again in trouble with the police and she asked me to help her."

"Help her? In what way?"

They had come to the end of the square. Brewster waited till they had crossed the road before answering.

"She said she wanted to go into hiding, to disappear for four or five days. She knew I had a cottage in the country, I'd often talked about it, and — well you can guess the rest. I arranged to meet her at the cottage. She said she'd be there by eight o'clock. I waited until midnight but she didn't show up. And that's the whole story so far as I'm concerned. The beginning, the middle and the end. Except that I'm fond of Jill and I'd like to know what the devil she's got herself mixed up in this time."

"You say you stayed at the cottage until midnight. What did you do then?"

"I drove back to Town."

Sam put a hand on Brewster's arm, steered him towards

the entrance to the coffee shop. It was still early for the coffee break and they found a table where they could talk without being overheard.

"Coffee for you?" Sam inquired as a girl in jeans came sauntering over to take their order. Brewster nodded.

"Two coffees, please."

"Capucinos?"

"Yes. Big cups, please."

The girl nodded but made no promises.

"Where's this cottage of yours?" Sam asked, as soon as the girl had disappeared.

"It's in Suffolk."

"Did you see anyone, talk to anyone, while you were there?"

"No. The cottage is fairly isolated. That's why I bought it."

"What did you do between eight o'clock and midnight?"

"What did I do?"

"Yes. Watch television?"

"No, I read. Or rather, I tried to read. As a matter of fact I was damned annoyed."

"You thought, 'Here we go, she's stood me up again!' "

Brewster grinned, "That's exactly what I thought!"

"Well, thank you for putting me in the picture. You needn't have done so, but in view of what happened I'm glad you did."

"Tell me, is Jill's condition serious?" Brewster leant forward on the table, his face worried. "I mean, really serious? I telephoned the hospital but they were very non-committal."

"I understand she's suffering from shock more than anything else. But the doctor seems to think she'll be all right."

"My God, I hope so," Brewster said fervently.

Surprisingly quickly the girl had brought them two steaming cups with white, creamy foam on top. Sam helped himself to sugar and stirred his cup.

"Mr Brewster, when I last saw you I questioned you about your clients — "

"You asked me if a man called Hogarth was a client of ours and I said he wasn't."

"Do you keep a record, a list of clients?"

"Regular clients, yes. But I know most of them by name anyway. Why?"

"Is Walter Randell a client of yours?"

"Walter Randell?" Brewster's head was bent as he raised his cup to his lips. "I don't think so. Although the name — Wait a minute!" He put the cup back on its saucer. "A rather distinguished looking chap; well dressed, wears glasses, always seems to be fiddling with them?"

"Yes, that's Randell."

"He's not a client but curiously enough I've met him."

"Where did you meet him?"

"I met him at the Leopard Club, about a week ago. He was playing roulette. And was he winning! I've never seen so much loot."

The coffee was still too hot to drink. Sam pulled out his cigarettes, offered Brewster one. Brewster shook his head.

"Who introduced you to him?"

"I can't remember. It was at a party. In fact, I don't think anyone introduced us, we just got talking." Brewster snapped his fingers. "I remember! I asked him if he always won and he said, 'I try very hard not to lose, Mr Brewster.'"

"Yes, that sounds like Randell. He knew your name then?"

"Yes, he did, come to think of it. But why are you interested in Walter Randell?"

"I'm not sure, but I think he's a friend of Jill's. And by a strange coincidence his wife, or rather ex-wife, lives next door to where my parents lived."

Sam had a meeting that morning at his literary agent's office in Russell Square. On the way home by underground he got out at Knightsbridge. There was still an hour before lunch-time and he wanted to settle a question that had been nagging at his mind.

The "Prince Hal" was a popular pub in a street opening off Brompton Road. It was always thronged from mid-day onwards. Sam pushed his way into the saloon bar, smiling amicably as he firmly elbowed a way between groups of people talking at the tops of their voices. To judge by his expression he was looking for a friend he expected to meet there.

As to who that friend might be Sam had kept an open mind. He'd run a quick eye over most of the customers and was just coming to the conclusion that he'd drawn blank when he saw a tubby little man with a balding head climbing down from a stool at the extreme end of the bar. Sam had pushed his way close before the man threw a pound note down on the bar. The barmaid, a massive blonde with a stupendous cleavage, picked it up and turned to the till.

"Keep the change, Wendy."

"Thank you, Mr Corby."

Corby nodded magnanimously. He put a match to the cigar he was holding, turned round and cannoned into Sam.

"Sorry, mate." He glanced up and saw Sam's face. His air of confident bonhomie evaporated. "Oh. Hello."

"Hello, Mr Corby." Sam greeted him as an old friend. "How are you?"

"I'm — I'm fine, thank you."

"Didn't expect to find you in this part of the world."

"Didn't expect to see you either," Corby grinned.

Sam winked at the barmaid. "Wendy's an old friend of mine."

"There's a sale room round the corner and I do business with them," Corby explained, " — or rather, I try to do business with them. Difficult people." He glanced round nervously and lowered his voice. "Is there any news?"

"News?"

"About my film?"

"Superintendent Bellamy's making inquiries. You'll be hearing from him."

Corby nodded, his sharp little eyes scanning Sam's face.

"Well — if you're ever looking for anything in the furniture line, give me a buzz. Bye, Wendy!"

He gave the barmaid a wave, checked that his wallet was safe in his pocket, then began to burrow his way through the crowd.

"Goodbye, Mr Corby." Wendy called after him. "And thank you."

Sam slid onto the stool vacated by Corby. "Hello, Wendy."

"Quite a stranger." Wendy gave him a warm smile as she wiped spilt beer off the counter.

"Yes. How have you been keeping?"

"Oh, not too bad, considering."

"How's the boy?"

"He's fine." Wendy could not conceal her motherly pride. "Growing up. Makes me feel a hundred at times, but there you are!" She put on a serious look and lowered her voice. "I was very sorry to hear about your mother and father. Quite upset me, it did — "

"Yes, well — "

She saw his shoulders droop and quickly changed the subject.

"What can I get you, sir? The usual? A tomato juice?"

"No. I'll have a gin and tonic."

"My word, we are living it up! What next, I wonder?"

She turned her buxom back to draw a measure of Gordon's from the rack of upturned bottles, then stooped for a bottle of tonic.

"Is Mr Corby one of your regulars?" Sam asked her, as she expertly removed the cap and poured half the bottle into his gin.

"Not really. I suppose he drops in about once a fortnight. He's in the antique business and there's a sale-room round the corner."

"Yes, so he said. Is he always on his own?"

"No, there's usually someone with him." She added ice and a slice of lemon and pushed the glass towards him. "He's very friendly with a chap called Morgan. I think it's Phil Morgan. Do you know him?" Sam shook his head. "Thick set, black beard. Horrible little devil. Drinks vodka like water and can't keep his hands to himself. I've told the Guv'nor if he touches me again I'll clobber him."

Sam laughed. Being clobbered by Wendy would be an unforgettable experience.

"Have you seen *The Daily World* this morning?"

"No, I never see a paper on a morning. By the time I've got his lordship off to school, done the washing up, and put me mask on, there isn't time to turn round — let alone read a newspaper."

Sam took a folded sheet of newspaper from his pocket. He pointed to the head and shoulders photograph.

"I'd like you to take a look at this girl. Her name's Jill Foster."

Wendy leant her bosom on the counter to study the picture more clearly.

"Jill Foster?"

"Yes. Do you know her?"

"No, but I've seen her."

"In here?"

"Yes. She's been in here several times. Once with that little horror I was telling you about. Phil Morgan."

There was a flower shop a few doors away from the "Prince Hal". Sam bought a bunch of chrysanthemums before hailing a taxi. The trip to his flat took only a few minutes. He asked the driver to wait while he went up to collect Jill Foster's handbag. On his previous visits to the hospital he had noticed how difficult it was to park anywhere round there. When the driver set him down at the main entrance ten minutes later he saw that he had made the right decision. There wasn't a parking space to be seen and a couple of traffic wardens were working their way through the cars parked on the yellow lines.

The girl at the reception desk was a stranger and he did not recognise any of the nurses hurrying to and fro. He was about to state his business when he saw the familiar figure of Dr Majduli. The Indian was living up to the claim that he was permanently on duty. If possible the shadows round his eyes were even darker, but he produced a welcoming smile when Sam crossed the hall to interrupt him.

"Hello, Superintendent. Nice to see you again. And how are you today?"

"I'm well, thank you. And Miss Foster?"

The doctor took Sam's arm and began to lead him down the corridor.

"She wasn't feeling too good first thing this morning, but I'm glad to say there's been an improvement. Your colleague, Superintendent Bellamy, didn't exactly cheer her up, I'm afraid. Would you like to see her?"

"Yes, if it's possible."

"She's got someone with her at the moment, but — "

"A visitor?"

"Yes, a girl friend. But if you're prepared to wait five or ten minutes — "

"Yes, of course."

They had reached the recess off the corridor which was used as a waiting room. Dr Majduli waved a hand at the chairs.

"Make yourself comfortable. Shall I ask the Sister to take care of those flowers?"

"If you would. And this is Miss Foster's handbag."

Dr Majduli accepted the flowers and handbag. "I'll see she gets it."

Sam sat down in the same chair as he had occupied on his previous visit. He chided himself for not remembering to bring something to read. Absent-mindedly he groped in his pocket for cigarettes, then saw a woman frowning fiercely at him from a seat opposite. He remembered that smoking was forbidden. There was no point in looking through the well-thumbed magazines on the table, but someone had left a book face downwards on one of the chairs. There was something familiar about it. He picked it up, then smiled as he saw the illustration on the cover.

He sat down again and began to turn the pages. It was odd that one could become so absorbed in one's own book. He did not notice that a woman had come up and stopped beside him till she spoke.

"Excuse me. That's my book."

Sam looked up. First he saw the light brown leather coat, then the blonde head of the woman who had given him such a detailed account of Larry Voss's death.

"Your book?" he said, completely taken aback.

"Yes, I left it in here."

"Oh." Sam closed the book and handed it to her.

"Thank you," she said, smiling.

"I — I saw you last night, in Pimlico. You spoke to me."

"That's right." She seemed quite unruffled by this encounter. "Perhaps I should introduce myself, Mr Harvey. I'm Chris Morris."

"Chris Morris!" It took Sam a moment to readjust to this statement. "Then it was you who wrote that article about me and Jill Foster?"

"Jill's a friend of mine. By sheer coincidence I was driving past the hospital when the ambulance arrived. I could hardly believe it when one of the nurses told me it was Jill — "

Sam stood up. Even then he was only a couple of inches taller than her.

"And was it coincidence that you happened to be in Pimlico last night when Larry Voss was murdered? Was he also a friend of yours?"

"No." She shook her head emphatically. "I'd never even heard of him till last night."

"Then what were you doing near his flat?"

"I was tailing someone."

"And the person you were tailing just happened to visit Pimlico the night Voss was murdered?" Sam said, not trying to hide his disbelief. "Is that it?"

"That's it." She smiled back at him.

"Who was this person?"

"Can't you guess? I was tailing you. I've been tailing you for the past three days."

Before Sam had time to become really angry a nurse appeared at the entrance to the waiting area.

"Superintendent Harvey? If you'll come this way I'll take you to Miss Foster."

"Thank you, nurse." Sam turned back to the reporter. "I won't be long. Please wait for me here. I'd very much like to continue this conversation."

There were only three beds in the ward where Jill lay. For the moment the other two were empty. Jill was sitting, well propped up by pillows, but still very uncomfortable and ill at ease. She was pale and there were shadows under her eyes. Her handbag was on the table by her bed. Sam's flowers had already been arranged in one of the hospital vases.

The nurse patted the pillows behind her head and picked up her water jug to fill it.

"Are you all right, my dear?"

"Yes, thank you."

"I'll be back shortly, but if you should want me just ring — "

She gave Sam an admonishing look as if warning him to be gentle with her patient, then went out of the room.

"Thank you for the flowers."

Jill at last brought her eyes up to Sam. He stood at the bottom of the bed looking down at her.

"How do you feel?"

"Oh, I don't know. Better than I did, I suppose."

"I've just been talking to a friend of yours."

"A friend of — oh, Chris."

"Yes."

"Do you know Chris then?"

"We've just met, in the waiting room. Have you read the article she wrote?"

"No, but she told me she was going to write one. Have you seen it?"

"Yes. Let's just say it isn't strictly accurate." To spare

her the strain of looking up at him Sam sat down in the chair beside her bed. "I understand you told Bellamy that you didn't actually see the man who attacked you."

"Yes," she answered uneasily. "That's true."

"Well, I've got news for you. It was a man called Larry Voss."

She reacted too quickly, avoiding his eye. "I've never heard of anyone called — "

"Jill, wait a minute." Sam cut in warningly. "Voss is dead. He was murdered."

Her mouth dropped open and her head jerked round. "Voss — dead?" she whispered.

"Yes. Didn't your friend Chris Morris tell you about it?"

"No, she didn't." Sam thought he detected an expression of relief on her face. "But — what happened?"

"He was killed. Last night."

"Who killed him?"

"I don't know. I was hoping you'd be able to tell me."

"So many people hated Voss, he had so many enemies." She said this as if talking to herself, then added: "I'm sorry I can't help you."

The nurse's face appeared for a moment in the small glass window in the door, then vanished again.

"All right, let's forget Voss and talk about another friend of yours."

"Voss wasn't a friend of mine!" she corrected him angrily.

"But Peter Brewster is, I take it. Is it true that you went to him for help?"

"Is that what Peter told you?"

"Never mind what he told me. Is it true?"

"Yes, it is. I was worried." She paused, then finished the sentence lamely. "And I thought perhaps he could help me."

"In what way did you think he could help you?"

"I wanted to — well, disappear for a little while. I knew he had a cottage in the country and I thought perhaps I might be able to persuade him into letting me stay there."

She glanced at him to see how he was taking this explanation.

"Did you persuade him?"

"Yes, I did. He said I could borrow the cottage for as long as I wanted. I arranged to meet him there last night. We were going to spend the weekend together."

Casually Sam produced from his pocket the book-matches he had found in her handbag. While continuing to talk he turned them over and over in his right hand without opening them.

"Why did you want to go into hiding?"

"I told you. I was in trouble. I still am."

"With the police?"

"Yes. Well, no — not just the police."

She had glanced casually at the book of matches, but completely without interest. He moved his chair round, facing her more directly.

"Jill — if you'll tell me the truth — if you're prepared to tell me to what extent you're mixed up in this affair, I'll do everything I can to help you."

"Yes, I know. You've said that before. You can't help me. No-one can."

"Please, let me be the judge of that. Why did you want to disappear? Who were you frightened of? Was it Voss?"

She nodded. He realised that she was still frightened, even though the man was dead.

"Only Voss? Sooner or later you've got to talk to me. You might as well talk to me now."

"I don't want to talk. Please leave me, I'm not feeling very well."

She reached for the bell on the end of its lead and pressed the knob. Sam stood up.

"I'm sorry you're not feeling well, I didn't mean to upset you. We'll talk some other time." He showed her the book-matches, turning the picture on the front towards her. "Oh, by the way, I found this in your handbag."

"They're not mine," she said quickly.

"Surely they must be yours," he insisted quietly.

"I hardly ever use matches. I have a lighter."

"Yes, I know. But this isn't a book of matches."

For the first time she gave the book-matches a careful look.

"This was in my handbag?"

"Yes."

"Where was the bag? Where did you find it?"

"It was on the floor near the settee. You must have dropped it when you were attacked."

She took the book-matches from him and studied the photo of the "Prince Hal".

"I've never seen this before. I can only imagine someone must have put it in my handbag."

"When?"

"I don't know when," she said impatiently. "I can't imagine. Unless Voss returned to the flat after we left for the hospital."

Sam nodded at the photo and the message, 'your friendly pub'. "Have you ever been to this pub — the Prince Hal?"

"No, never. I don't even know where it is."

"Open it, look inside."

She opened the book of matches and did not seem particularly surprised that it was empty.

Sam said, "What about those phone numbers?"

"They don't mean anything to me, and I've already told

you, more than once — I don't know anyone called Hogarth." He took the book of matches from her and began tapping them with the back of his fingers. "What does that mean? Don't you believe me?"

"I'm trying very hard to believe you," he said.

"I've told you the truth. I can't do more than that."

Sam glanced towards the door, listening for the sound of the nurse's feet in the corridor outside. He knew he had not much time left.

"Then tell me the truth about my mother and father. Where exactly did you take them after you picked them up at the airport?"

"I can't remember."

"You said you took them to a house, outside London."

"I can't remember."

"Where was this house?"

"I've told you — I can't remember!"

"You were going to tell me. You would have told me if it hadn't been for Voss."

"Please! Please leave me alone — " Her face suddenly twisted with pain. She eased herself carefully back against the pillows.

"All right, Jill. I'm sorry. If you change your mind and want to talk to me, just tell the doctor." He went to the door then stopped just short of it. "Oh, forgive me, but before I go there is one other question I'd like to ask you. Why did you take the boy to Pennymore?"

"Boy? What boy?" Her eyes were wide with bewilderment. "And what on earth is Pennymore?"

"It's a house near Guildford where my parents lived. When my father made an offer for it he kept saying not a penny more. The name stuck."

Her face was blank. The name had produced no reaction from her. She did not smile at the innocent pun.

"You don't know what I'm talking about?"

"No, I'm afraid I don't."

"It's not important." He smiled at her. "I hope you'll soon feel better."

As he put his hand on the door-knob it opened with a jerk, almost hitting him on the nose. The nurse swept in. With her sleeves rolled up to the elbow she seemed prepared to chuck Sam out by the seat of his trousers.

"Did you ring for me?" she demanded, glaring not at Jill but at Sam.

"Yes, but it doesn't matter now. I'm sorry, Nurse."

"I'm just leaving," Sam explained meekly.

"That woman you were talking to — " The nurse managed to imply that Sam's conversation with Chris Morris had been highly improper.

"Yes?"

"She asked me to tell you she's sorry but she had to leave. She said she'd try and telephone you. I said I'd give you the message."

He thanked her with suitable humility and slipped rapidly out through the door.

Jill's friends and acquaintances were evidently making the most of the brief visiting hours allowed by the hospital. As he was going out through the main hall Sam spotted Peter Brewster coming in. He was wearing a different but equally immaculate suit. His hands were fully occupied with a big bunch of flowers and a gift-wrapped box.

"Hello, Mr Brewster," Sam hailed him.

Brewster paused and came towards him anxiously.

"Have you seen Jill?"

"Yes, I've just left her."

"How is she?"

"She's not too bad, considering."

"I called here yesterday, soon after I saw you. The doctor wouldn't let me see her."

"I don't think she was feeling too good yesterday."

Brewster glanced round quickly to satisfy himself that no-one was standing near enough to hear what was said.

"Superintendent, since we had our conversation I've been thinking about all those questions you asked me and I decided that next time I saw you I'd put my cards on the table. Do you think it was me who attacked Jill? Because if you do — "

"We know who attacked her. It was a man called Larry Voss."

"But Voss is dead. It was on the radio."

"I imagine it was. Did you know Voss?"

"I met him once. He came to the garage." Brewster's eyes were on a stretcher-trolley being wheeled across the hall. "He wanted to see Jill but she was out on a job. We stood talking — about cars, if I remember rightly. He had a Lotus and was thinking of selling it."

"Why did he want to see Jill?"

"I don't know why. He didn't say and I didn't ask him." Brewster put his hand on Sam's arm. "Harvey, tell me — what sort of trouble is Jill in? Is she frightened of something?"

"She hasn't confided in me."

"But you must have some idea."

"Both my parents were murdered," Sam said flatly. "I think Jill knows who murdered them and why it happened."

Brewster was shocked. He shook his head.

"But I had a long talk to Jill about your parents — it was after you interviewed her at the restaurant. She said she'd never seen either of them until she picked them up at Waterloo."

"I don't think she was telling you the truth."

"Look," Brewster put on a great show of making up his mind. "I'll put my cards on the table — "

"I thought you had done, Mr Brewster," Sam reminded him with a faint smile.

"Last night I suddenly realised, for the first time, just how fond I am of Jill. If she really is in trouble I want to help her." Once again he put a hand on Sam's arm but had to remove it to prevent the gift parcel slipping from under his arm. "Please believe me, I'll do anything to help her. I really will."

"Then get her to change her mind."

"Change her mind? About what?"

"Jill picked my parents up at London Airport and took them to a house somewhere outside London."

"Did she tell you that?"

"Yes, but unfortunately before she could tell me where the house was Larry Voss arrived on the scene."

"I see. And now, I take it, she refuses to talk?"

"If you really are fond of her, Mr Brewster," Sam told him very seriously, "Believe me — you'd be well advised to persuade her to talk."

Back at his flat Sam managed to put in two hours at his desk before his visitor arrived. Bellamy was soaking wet, having walked most of the way from Victoria Street in the interests of physical fitness. The fact that it was pouring with rain had not deterred him in the slightest. He hung his dripping raincoat, hat and umbrella up in the hall. It was clear that this was going to be no fleeting visit. Sam determined to put the best face on it.

"You look as if you could use a drink. What about a Scotch to warm the cockles of your heart?"

"No, thanks. I don't drink whisky."

"Gin and tonic, then?"

"Just a tonic, thanks. No gin."

Sam was shaking his head as he went into the kitchen. What was the point of keeping fit if you could not enjoy the good things of life?

When he came back, a glass of tonic water in one hand and a stiff scotch in the other, Bellamy had ensconced himself in an easy chair. He was using his handkerchief to wipe the rain off his face.

Sam handed him his glass and raised his own.

"Skol!"

Bellamy tasted his drink gingerly as if he suspected Sam of doctoring it.

"I rather imagine you know why I'm here."

"You want to talk to me about Voss?"

"Amongst other things. Why did you visit Voss the night he was murdered?"

"I heard Jill Foster call out a name just before she was attacked. Later I realised the name was Voss."

"So?"

"So I thought it was about time I made the gentleman's acquaintance."

Bellamy put his glass down and shook out the soaking bottoms of his trouser legs.

"Didn't it occur to you that the correct thing to do was to contact me?"

Sam had perched himself on the edge of the desk.

"Yes, it did occur to me, but I felt that you had quite enough on your plate at the moment."

"Look, Harvey. I don't wish to be difficult. I know how you must feel, but *I* am in charge of this investigation."

"I know you are, Bellamy, and I'll help you in any way I can. What would you like me to do?"

"Well, to start with, I'd like you to be a little less patronising, and a little more co-operative."

Sam raised his eyebrows, then did his best to look more co-operative.

"What's on your mind, Bellamy?"

"I want some information and you're the only one who can give it to me. I understand your father worked for one of the big insurance companies?"

"That's right. He retired about four years ago."

"On a pension?"

"Yes."

Bellamy stopped fiddling with his trousers and looked up.

"Would you say your father was a wealthy man?"

"Good heavens, no! Not by any stretch of the imagination."

"Well off?"

"No, I wouldn't even say he was well off. Not by today's standards. My mother inherited a certain amount of money when her brother died."

"What do you imagine your father was worth?"

"I really don't know."

"Hazard a guess. Twenty thousand — thirty thousand — forty — "

Puzzled now by Bellamy's line of questioning Sam took a drink of whisky and thought before answering.

"Probably about twenty, excluding Pennymore. That's the house my parents lived in."

"Which was bought, when?"

"Oh — about twenty-five years ago. But I'll know more about my father's affairs tomorrow morning. I'm meeting his lawyer."

"Who are his lawyers?"

"A firm called Adams, Smith and Gilbert. George

115

Adams, the senior partner, was by way of being a friend of my father's."

"Harvey, tell me: why did your parents travel up to London instead of going straight to Heathrow? Surely, from Guildford, there was no need for them to come to London. You could have met them at the airport."

It was a good question. Sam had wondered the same thing more than once as he had gone again and again over the last hours he had spent with his parents.

"I don't know why they came to London. Probably because my mother wanted to spend more time with me."

"Forgive my asking, but — were you on good terms with your parents?"

"With my mother, certainly."

"And your father?"

Bellamy on the job was not such a figure of fun. These questions were coming very near the knuckle. Sam slid off the desk and moved round to the side table where he had left his cigarettes.

"Well, to be truthful — there were times when my father and I didn't always see eye to eye."

"In what way didn't you see eye to eye?"

"He was very much a loner."

"Aren't you a loner, Harvey?"

"Yes, I am — but in not quite the same way. There were times when he — "

Sam took a cigarette from the pack and put it in his mouth. Without thinking he offered one to his visitor. Bellamy shook his head with emphatic disapproval. He was one of those people who are not content with giving up smoking themselves but carry on a war of silent attrition against all those who yield to that lamentable habit. Sam got his cigarette going, but he cruised round behind Bellamy's chair, ostensibly to collect an ashtray.

"There's something I have to explain to you, Bellamy. It's not going to be very easy. Jason Harvey was my step-father. My own father was killed when I was two years old."

"But — " Bellamy swivelled round in his chair. "Then your name's not really Harvey?"

"I'll explain. Mother and I were alone till I reached the age of eight. Then she met Jason. I was glad for her sake when they got married. I was old enough to realise how lonely she was. Meg was born a year later. It was then that I started calling myself Sam Harvey. It saved a lot of awkward questions and stopped me from feeling the odd one out."

Bellamy was not so insensitive as Sam had thought. After that first inquiring glance he had kept his eyes to the front, realising that it was difficult for Sam to tell all this.

"Later I regretted it. I felt that in a way I had betrayed my father. That's why I joined the police, but I did so for all the wrong reasons."

"I can't see why — " Bellamy began, then checked himself.

"My father was a policeman. He was shot trying to stop a couple of bank robbers escaping."

This time Bellamy's head did jerk round. "Roger Kaye," he said quietly. "Lloyds Bank case. Manchester. The bastards got life."

Sam nodded.

"I see," Bellamy said. He imbibed some more tonic water. "That explains a good many things."

"I did my best to like Jason. He could be very friendly, very helpful and yet I always felt a barrier between us. Of course, Meg was the apple of his eye and I was very fond of her too. That was the only real bond between us. Bellamy, you'll keep this to yourself, won't you? I'm only telling you in case it's relevant to your inquiries."

"I will as long as I can. But it may have to come out. What about your mother? How did she feel about all this?"

"She worshipped Father, she really did. I don't think there was anything she wouldn't have done for him. 'What's good enough for Jason is good enough for Hannah.' Believe it or not, she actually used to say that to us."

"Well, your step-father was certainly an attractive man."

"Since Meg was born I've always called him Father. I'm not going to start referring to him as step-father now that he's dead. Did you know him?"

"No, but curiously enough, when I saw that film the other day I suddenly realised that I'd seen him before somewhere. I couldn't recall where it was, then last night, just as I was doing my exercises, I remembered. I saw him at the Leopard."

"At the Leopard?" Sam echoed in astonishment. "You can't mean the club in Mayfair."

"I do."

"Surely you're mistaken?"

"I'm not mistaken. I have a very good memory for faces. Besides, I've made inquiries. It was your — it was Jason Harvey."

Sam came round the chair so that he could see Bellamy's face.

"I find this very difficult to believe. What on earth would my father be doing in a place like that?"

"Well," Bellamy said drily, "the night I saw him he was thoroughly enjoying himself."

"Was he alone?"

"No. He had someone with him. Someone you know. Mrs Randell."

Sam shook his head in disbelief. "My father was with Margaret Randell at the Leopard Club?"

"That's right. They were having dinner together. Later they danced and if my memory serves me right they played baccarat."

"The Leopard." Sam stubbed his cigarette out in the ashtray he had been carrying round. "That's run by a woman."

"Katie Mellowfield. She's the last person on earth you'd expect to find running a night club."

"What were you doing at the Leopard, Bellamy?" Sam challenged.

"Drinking tonic waters." Bellamy gave one of his rare smiles and put down the empty glass. "You say you're seeing this lawyer tomorrow morning. What's the name again?"

"George Adams."

"And he was a friend of Jason Harvey. A close friend?"

"Fairly close. They used to play golf together."

Bellamy stood up. The neat crease in his trousers was ruined.

"Question him about your step-father. Be frank with him. Ask him about Margaret Randell. See what he says. He may be able to throw some light on the Leopard affair."

As Bellamy moved out to the hall Sam said casually, "I saw Jill Foster this afternoon."

"Yes, so I gather. It's funny, you know, I started by disliking that girl, but she's rather won me over."

"Had you met her before?"

"Before?" Bellamy was surprised by the question. "Before what?"

"Before they put you on the case?"

He stopped, one hand outstretched to take his raincoat off the hook.

"No. Why do you ask?"

"I wondered, that's all." Back in the sitting-room the phone began to ring. "Will you excuse me?"

"Yes, of course. I'll see myself out."

As he picked up the telephone Sam could hear the rustling noise of Bellamy putting on his black rubberised mackintosh.

"Hello. Harvey speaking."

"Mr Harvey, this is Chris Morris."

"Oh, hello, Miss Morris."

"Mrs Morris," she corrected. "You got my message?"

"Yes, I did."

"I'm sorry I had to dash away like that. I suddenly remembered I had an appointment in Fleet Street."

"I'd like to continue our conversation. What about tomorrow afternoon?"

"Tomorrow evening would suit me better. Shall we say six o'clock?"

"Yes, that's fine. Since you've been tailing me, I rather imagine you have my address."

"Yes, I have. But I suggest you come to my place. Hubert, my husband, is dying to meet you. You'll find you have a great deal in common, Mr Harvey."

"Yes, all right." Slightly puzzled by her remark, he pulled the telephone pad and pencil towards him. "What's your address?"

"We have a flat in the Boltons. It's on the south side of the gardens. Number 28A. We shall look forward to seeing you."

Sam dropped the pencil. That was an address he would have no problem remembering.

"Thank you for ringing," he said.

Thoughtfully he replaced the receiver. From the hall came the tell-tale click of the latch as his front door was quietly closed.

6

A few miles short of Guildford Sam pulled in at a garage which he knew from experience sold petrol at a lower price than any other in the neighbourhood. When the forecourt attendant had replaced the cap on the petrol tank Sam asked him to check the oil. The man showed him the dipstick.

"She'll take about half a litre, sir."

"Just about," Sam agreed. "Check the battery level while you're at it, will you?"

While the attendant peeled the seal off a tin of oil, Sam took a cloth from the glove pocket of the Porsche and started to clean his windscreen. A Rolls Royce swung into the forecourt and drew up on the other side of the row of pumps. It was a fawn Silver Spirit, driven by a chauffeur in a grey livery. The Porsche seemed very small beside it.

The garage proprietor himself came hurrying out to deal with the Rolls. While the chauffeur gave his instructions the car's passenger opened the rear door and stepped out, presumably to stretch his legs. Sam glanced up out of curiosity and caught him in the act of readjusting his spectacles on the bridge of his nose.

"Morning, Mr Randell," he called, across the bonnet of his car.

Walter Randell was very dapper this morning and much more sure of himself than when he had come to visit Sam. Perhaps the Rolls Royce gave him confidence.

"Why, hello Superintendent. This is a surprise! What are you doing in this part of the world?"

"I've got an appointment in Guildford." Sam threw the

cloth onto the seat of his car and went round to shake hands with Randell.

"I've just come from there. I had an appointment too." Randell paused, then added wryly, "With my wife."

"How is Mrs Randell — or shouldn't I ask?"

"Ask by all means," Randell invited, very ironic. "But the answer, I regret to say, is unprintable. 'Destructive, damnable, deceitful woman!' Who was it said that?"

"Congreve or Thomas Otway, I'm not sure which."

"Well, whoever it was, he was dead right." He adjusted his glasses again. "I just can't get to grips with Margaret, I really can't. One minute she wants a divorce, the next minute she doesn't. One minute she agrees to a settlement — providing there's no publicity, of course, because she's a very private sort of person — and the next minute she's threatening to talk to the *News of the World*!" Sam laughed, but Randell kept a straight face. "If you ask me, the only person she ever really got along with was your father."

"How friendly was she with my father, Mr Randell?" Sam kept his tone casual.

"How friendly?" The question had surprised Randell. "Well — they were just good friends, so far as I know."

"Was she having an affair with him?"

"Good lord, no!" He thought for a moment, then said more carefully, "Well — I don't think so. It never occurred to me. Forgive me, but — whatever made you ask the question?"

"A friend of mine thought he saw the two of them having dinner together one night."

"That's possible, I suppose. But surely, that doesn't mean they were having an affair. Where did this friend of yours see them — in Guildford?"

"No. In London. They were at the Leopard Club."

"The Leopard Club?" Randell repeated the name with only slightly less astonishment than Sam had done when Bellamy mentioned it.

"Yes. Do you know it?"

"Of course I know it! Well, I'm damned! I only met your father once, very briefly, but I wouldn't have thought the Leopard Club quite his scene."

"Neither would I, Mr Randell."

"Don't get me wrong." Randell put a hand on Sam's arm. "It's a very respectable sort of club so far as those sort of places go. It's run by a woman called Katie Mellowfield."

"So I believe."

"Extraordinary woman. Always looks to me as if she should be in the Salvation Army." Randell put his head on one side and studied Sam quizzically as if he was trying to see the father in the son. "I wonder if Margaret really was having it off with your old man. You know, it just never occurred to me."

"That's thirteen pounds seventy-six altogether, sir," the attendant said, at Sam's elbow.

He nodded at Randell and turned away, reaching for his wallet.

Nothing had changed at Pennymore. The house still had that bereaved expression. The grass on the lawn was just a little bit longer. A few leaves had fallen from the tree where his swing had hung. The heavy rain had washed away any tyre marks which a visiting vehicle might have left.

This time when he opened the door he found four letters lying on the mat inside. He picked them up and closed the door behind him. Two of them were circulars. Of the others one was handwritten. He was trying to recognise the writing when the doorbell rang. He checked his watch. It was still five minutes short of eleven-thirty.

The caller was Margaret Randell. She must have been

watching from her front window to get here so quickly. He saw that she was a little flushed.

"Why, hello Margaret. Come along in."

"I saw your car," she said breathlessly. "I wondered if there was anything I could do?"

"No, but it's very kind of you. I was going to drop in on you, but I've got someone coming to see me at eleven-thirty."

"Oh, well, in that case I won't — " she began to turn away, but he held the door wider.

"That's all right. He's a lawyer, so ten to one he'll be late. Come in, please."

"There are some more letters in the living-room. I put them there last night."

He led the way into the sitting-room. There was a neat pile of correspondence on the bureau.

"I don't think there's anything of importance," she said. "Would you like me to forward letters? I could very easily re-address them."

"That's very kind of you, but I should hate to put you to any more trouble. You're doing enough for me as it is, looking after the house."

"Nonsense! It's no trouble, I assure you. Incidentally, what are you going to do about the house? Have you decided?"

He picked up the rest of the letters and began to look through them as he talked.

"I shall sell it. That's one of the things I want to talk to George Adams about."

"Well, whoever buys it, I only hope they turn out to be as nice as your mother and father."

"Margaret, may I ask you a very personal question?"

She blinked a little nervously then composed her face in readiness.

"I don't see why not."

"How friendly were you with my father?"

"How friendly?" She shook her head, an honest woman frankly puzzled. "I'm not sure I understand you. What are you suggesting?"

"I was told by a friend of mine that my father took you out to dinner one night. To the Leopard Club, of all places."

She laughed with what seemed to be genuine relief. "You can tell your friend — whoever he is — that he's been sadly misinformed. Your father did not take me out to dinner."

"He didn't?"

"The boot was on the other foot. I took your father. And, in case your friend takes it into his head to tell you his version of what happened, let me put the record straight. Your father had an appointment in London and since I wanted to do some shopping I begged a lift from him. On the way up to Town we started talking about restaurants and I asked him if he'd like to have dinner with me that evening. He'd been awfully kind to me, on more than one occasion, and I felt it was an ideal opportunity to repay him."

"And you chose the Leopard Club?"

She did not miss the sarcasm in his voice.

"Yes, I did," she said defiantly, "and for a very good reason. Katie Mellowfield, who runs the club, is a friend of mine. I used to go there with Walter in the old days. I hadn't seen Katie since Walter and I parted, and I knew she'd be delighted to see me again. I also had a shrewd idea that she wouldn't let us pay for our dinner. And I was right! That's precisely what happened."

"Talking of your husband, I bumped into him this morning on my way here. I gather he'd just left you?"

As always when her husband was mentioned the line of her lips hardened. She went restlessly towards the french windows.

"Yes, he'd just left me all right! What in God's name I ever saw in that man, I'll never know. He's quite the most insensitive creature I've ever met. He knows I'm pretty hard up these days so he spent the best part of an hour telling me how badly off *he* was! Then, just as he was leaving, he had the audacity to say: 'Margaret, do take a look at the new Rolls. It's super.' I could have killed him!" She turned about and came back to the middle of the room. "But don't let's talk about my husband. I've had enough of Walter for one day."

From somewhere at the back of the house a bell rang faintly.

"That's your visitor. I'll be off."

He accompanied her to the front door and opened it for her. A maroon-coloured Rover had drawn up behind the Porsche. The man standing on the doorstep was aged about fifty. He was hatless but wore a black overcoat with a velvet collar. A neat, dark moustache gave him a slightly military look. He was carrying a well-worn and bulging leather briefcase.

"Good morning, Sam. Sorry I'm late. Do apologise."

"Hello, George! Come along in."

"Shouldn't have taken that last phone call. Big mistake. Always is."

Adam's sharp eyes were making a quick assessment of Margaret Randell, who was sidling past him.

"I don't know whether you know Mrs Randell?" Sam said.

"No, I haven't had that pleasure."

Adams gave her a courtly bow, as Margaret switched on a formal smile.

126

"Go along in, George." Sam nodded towards the living-room. "I'll be with you in a minute."

"Thank you."

Adams nodded to Margaret, managing to convey the impression that he wished their meeting had lasted longer. She made no move to leave until the solicitor had gone into the house.

Then she said: "How's that girl getting along? The one we talked about on the telephone — "

"Jill Foster? She's better. I should imagine she'll be out of hospital in a week or so."

"The reason I ask is because I looked at the photograph, in the newspaper. It was the girl I saw, I'm pretty sure."

"You mean the girl with the boy?"

"Yes. She was driving the car." She turned to go down the two steps. "Perhaps you'd like to drop in later for a drink?"

"Thank you. I will, certainly, if I've got time."

In the living-room Adams was staring at a photograph of Jason and Hannah Harvey which stood on the desk. There was genuine sadness on his face as Sam came into the room.

"How are you, Sam?" he asked with concern.

"I'm all right, George. All things considered."

"You got my letter?"

"Yes, I did. It was a very nice letter. Thank you."

"I can't begin to tell you how much I miss Jason. We didn't see a great deal of each other during the past couple of years, but — "

"When was the last time you saw him?"

"Curiously enough, about a week before — " Adams broke off, searched for an appropriate word and then decided that some things are better left unsaid. "He came to the office one afternoon, quite unexpectedly, and handed

127

me an envelope. In fact, that's one of the reasons why I'm here." The solicitor put his briefcase on the settee and undid the catches. "Sam, unless I'm very much mistaken, you're going to be very surprised by what I'm going to tell you this morning."

"Surprised? In what way?"

"How much do you think your father was worth?"

"That's the second time I've been asked that question in the past twenty-four hours."

"Really?" Adams withdrew an envelope from the brief-case and straightened up. "Who asked the question? And what was your answer?"

"A colleague of mine asked it. I said my father was probably worth about twenty thousand pounds, not in-cluding this house."

"You're way out," Adams said quietly. He paused for effect. "Your father's estate is worth well over half a million."

"Half a million?" Bert Sinclair repeated Sam's words. "Half a million pounds sterling?"

"That's what he said."

"I'm amazed. I never for one moment thought your father — Were you surprised?"

"That's putting it mildly."

Bert Sinclair had suggested meeting Sam at a coffee shop near Harrods which sold very good cakes. The chief superintendent had a sweet tooth and a special weakness for chocolate and coffee eclairs. Ironically, despite a con-siderable corporation, he looked a great deal healthier than Bellamy. The two men had found a quiet table at the back of the room. As it was tea-time the place was rapidly filling up with women laden with the distinctive green Harrods bags.

Bert watched appreciatively as the waitress set down the tea-tray on which was a plate with half a dozen creamy cakes. As Sam poured out a couple of cups Bert helped himself to a chocolate eclair and sank his teeth into it.

"I suppose this chap Adams knows what he's talking about?" he said, after munching for a minute.

"He knows what he's talking about. Apart from being a very good lawyer he was a friend of my father's. You take sugar, Bert?"

"Yes. Four lumps. Correct me if I'm mistaken. Your father worked for an insurance company."

"That's right. World Wide Benefits."

"What was his salary, have you any idea?"

"When he retired he was getting about nine thousand a year."

"Then how on earth did he manage to accumulate half a million?"

Sam shrugged.

Bert wiped his lips and took a drink of tea. "Does the lawyer know?"

"He has no idea. He was flabbergasted when he discovered the size of the estate."

"When was the last time he saw Jason?"

"About a week before the murder. Apparently my father turned up at his office, unexpectedly. He had a sealed envelope with him which he wanted Adams to take care of."

"What was in the envelope, do you know?"

"Yes, I do."

One of the attractions of this place was that the tables were set in little alcoves separated by partitions about four foot high. Sam glanced over the top of the partition behind him. The next table was occupied by three ladies who were deep in a discussion about the length of skirts. Satisfied that no one was taking an interest in him and Bert, he pulled from his pocket a notebook with a leather cover. He pushed it across the table to Bert.

Bert put down the coffee eclair to which he had just helped himself. He wiped his fingers on the paper napkin before opening the notebook and slowly turning the pages. Each page was covered by a maze of letters and numerals.

"What do these mean?"

"Search me."

"Is it your father's handwriting?"

"Yes, it is. I imagine it's a cipher of some kind, but I can't make head or tail of it."

Bert bent his head closer to the book.

"Well, if it's a cipher, we'd better let that wizard Osgood take a look at it. If he can't make head or tail of it, no-one can. Do you mind if I take this back to the Yard?"

Not waiting for an answer Bert closed the notebook and slipped it into his own pocket. He picked up the eclair again.

"Was the envelope addressed to you?"

"No, it wasn't addressed to anyone. It simply had my father's initials on it."

"I take it your father didn't tell his lawyer what was in it?"

"No, he didn't."

Sam raised his cup to his lips with both hands. He had not been tempted by the creamy cakes. He watched Bert demolish the eclair in four healthy mouthfuls. The chief superintendent glanced up and grinned like a naughty boy.

"Do you know what I think, Bert?" Sam said. "That's why my flat was searched. They were looking for the notebook."

"Could be, Sam." Bert appeared to be waging an internal battle with his conscience. His conscience lost. He helped himself to another cake.

28A The Boltons was a well-favoured house with a dozen steps leading up to a Georgian style front door. Like practically every house in the neighbourhood it had been converted to flats. This time there was no intercom from the front door to the individual flats. He was searching for some indication of which floor the Morrises lived on when the heavy black door was opened by a young man.

"Mr Harvey? Hubert Morris. Saw you out of the window. Do come in."

His voice was breathless, perhaps from rushing down the stairs. He seemed young to be the husband of the blonde newspaper reporter. He had an eager but vulnerable look with slightly popping eyes. He wore a denim suit of dark blue and a carelessly tied scarlet neckerchief that looked like a piece of dress material discarded by his wife.

He took Sam by the arm and led him into the tiled hall. A wide staircase with a fine banister wound upwards. There was no lift.

"We're upstairs — on the first floor." Hubert kept glancing at Sam with a secretive smile. Sam wondered if they could have met before and Hubert was waiting to be recognised.

He bounded up the stairs, outpacing Sam, and stood by the open door of the flat waiting for him to catch up.

"Chris is out, but she'll be back soon," he burbled on, as Sam entered. "Expecting her any minute. Now what would you like to drink. Don't say Scotch because we haven't got any."

Sam had stopped and was gazing round the big living

room. It faced north and had lofty uncurtained windows. There was an elegant and purposeful untidiness about the place which was oddly attractive.

"Er — "

"Beer — gin and tonic? Gin and tonic — beer?"

"Thank you. I'll have a gin and tonic."

"Splendid! Dead easy — I hope. Be with you in a tick. Take a pew."

With amusement Sam watched him prance like a ballet dancer to a door and disappear through it. There wasn't a seat in the room that was uncluttered by books. In the far corner stood an easel with a canvas on it. There was a desk-like piece of furniture containing artist's equipment and paraphernalia. Piles of books had been placed round a table to form stools. On the walls was a selection of extremely interesting lithographs, etchings, prints and original drawings. Sam was examining these when Hubert's head popped round the door.

"Ice?"

"Er — please."

"Slice of lemon?"

"If you've got it."

"Good point!" Hubert stabbed a finger in Sam's direction and vanished again.

He could hear Hubert hunting wildly for the lemon as he continued his tour. He had almost made a complete circuit before his host reappeared with two glasses balanced on an old chess-board.

"Did you do these?" Sam waved a hand at the pictures.

"Only the good ones." He grinned and handed Sam a glass.

"Thank you. They all seem good to me, but I'm not an expert."

"But you know what you like."

Sam wondered if Hubert was being sarcastic in producing the old cliché. He shot a look at his host. Hubert grinned and raised his glass.

"Cheers!"

"Skol!" Sam took a drink and then involuntarily looked at his glass.

" 'Fraid it's vodka. Out of gin," Hubert explained. He took Sam's arm again and led him to the far corner of the room behind the easel.

"Come over here and I'll show you my favourite. I feel sure you'll like it."

Sam allowed himself to be conducted round the easel. On a section of the wall hung a large watercolour drawing. It was handsomely framed. Sam recognised it immediately. Hubert was watching him with an expectant smile on his face.

"Did you do this?" asked Sam.

Hubert nodded, his smile broadening. "Yes, it's the original. I hope you liked my jacket as much as I liked your book."

"I did indeed. I wrote to the publishers and said so. How did you find out I was the author?"

"I was afraid you were going to ask that. I was in the art director's office at your publishers one morning and you telephoned. Scofield was so damned secretive — insisted on taking the call in the outer office — I became suspicious. I told my wife about it and she made one or two inquiries. Chris was on the *Chicago Tribune* for four years so she's very good at making inquiries."

"So I've discovered."

The two men exchanged a smile.

"Was *Dinner at the Zoo* the first book you'd written?"

"No, but it was the first one I didn't tear up."

After an affectionate glance at his picture Hubert moved

133

back into the centre of the room, avoiding an open portfolio of drawings which had been left on the floor.

"How on earth you managed to write a book like that while you were still with the police, I'll never know."

"*Still* with the police?" Sam said quickly.

"Yes. Forgive me, but — aren't you retiring from Scotland Yard in order to write full time?"

"You seem to be very well informed, Mr Morris."

"Not me. My wife. But you didn't come here to talk about yourself, I'm sure. So forgive me." He went to the window and stood looking down into the street. Sam's Porsche was parked almost directly opposite. "I gather from Chris that you're interested in Jill Foster?"

"Very much so."

"An extraordinary girl. I'd like to have castrated that bastard Ross, or Voss."

"In what way is Jill Foster extraordinary?" Sam asked, surprised by Hubert's vehemence.

"Well, to start with — she saved my life."

"You mean — literally?"

Hubert nodded, his back still turned.

"Literally. A few months ago Chris and I suddenly decided — " He broke off and then his whole voice and manner brightened. "Ah, here's Chris now. She'll tell you all about it."

Sam moved to his shoulder so that he could see down into the street. A scarlet Metro had pulled into a parking space by the kerb about twenty yards further along. He saw Chris Morris, still wearing her distinctive leather overcoat, step out from the driving seat. She moved quickly round to the passenger's side to help someone to get out and to protect them from passing vehicles as they did so. Sam saw a boy of about twelve emerge. He was wearing

134

a school blazer and carrying a satchel. Chris slammed the door of the car and then anxiously led him round to the pavement.

As the two of them stepped up onto it and began to walk towards the steps of Number 28A he saw the reason for her solicitude. The boy had a noticeable limp.

7

When Chris Morris entered the room she was alone. She had taken off her overcoat and scarf. She was wearing a pale blue suit. A broad belt emphasised the slimness of her figure.

"I'm sorry to have kept you waiting, Mr Harvey. We've been rehearsing for our school play."

She gave Hubert a kiss on each cheek.

"How's it coming along, darling?"

"Well, Jonathan's going to be a most unusual Iago, to put it mildly. Go and say hello to him, Hubert. He's dying to tell you all about it."

As Hubert went out she quickly checked her reflection in a wall mirror and rearranged her hair.

"I've just been admiring your husband's work," Sam said.

"I hope you like it. I must confess I think he's awfully clever but then I'm prejudiced. Did you like the book jacket?"

"Very much." He waited till she turned round before asking, "Is that why you were tailing me – because of my book?"

She laughed. "Naturally I was intrigued when Hubert told me that he thought you'd written it. Scotland Yard detective writes children's best seller! But I was keeping an eye on you for quite a different reason. My editor heard a rumour that you'd resigned from the Yard and he asked me to find out if your resignation had anything to do with — recent events."

"My resignation had nothing to do with the death of my parents. I resigned before then, because I wanted to devote more time to writing."

"I see." She unzipped a pocket and withdrew a packet of cigarettes. "Why were your parents murdered, Mr Harvey?"

"Why don't you ask your friend Jill Foster that question?"

"I have."

"And what did she say?"

"She says she knows nothing about the affair. She simply picked your mother and father up at Waterloo and drove them to the airport."

"That isn't true." He shook his head at her offer of a cigarette. "She returned to Heathrow later the same day and picked up my parents for the second time."

"Are you sure?"

"I'm quite sure."

"Where did she take them?"

"To a house outside London."

"Where was this house?"

"I wish I knew, but she refuses to tell me." He watched her insert a cigarette in a holder and light it. "Mrs Morris, how long have you known Jill Foster?"

"About six months. We met under the most unusual circumstances. It was late one night and during a terrible storm."

"Is that when she saved your husband's life?"

"Did Hubert tell you about it?"

"He didn't tell me what happened."

"It's rather a long story, I'm afraid — "

Hubert had come back into the room. They exchanged a look full of parental pride and shared secrets.

"You tell him, darling."

Hubert needed no second bidding. Sam guessed that what he was about to hear was an oft-told story.

"For some time now we've been talking about buying a cottage. A weekend place. We've looked at various properties but so far we've been unlucky. About six months ago we drove out to see a place in Oxfordshire called — "

Hubert glanced at his wife for a cue. She had tossed the books off a chair onto the floor and was sitting with her legs stretched out.

"Daylight Cottage."

"That's right. Daylight Cottage. The estate agent warned us that it was in a pretty remote part of the country and that we'd probably have difficulty finding it. Anyway — to cut a long story short, we ran into a terrible storm and driving down a country lane the car skidded, hit a tree, and overturned. Both Chris and Jonathan finally managed to extricate themselves but I couldn't move. I was trapped — literally pinned beneath the car."

He paused dramatically. However unpleasant the experience had been at the time he was obviously deriving great satisfaction from it now. Chris took up the tale.

"Jonathan, poor darling, had hurt his foot and was hardly able to move. I was just about to leave him with his father and try and get help from somewhere when we heard a car approaching. There was a girl in the car. We found out later her name was Jill Foster."

"She was marvellous, absolutely marvellous," said Hubert. "In less than an hour we were in the local hospital."

"Where exactly did this accident happen, Mr Morris?"

"I think I'm right in saying the nearest village was called Heldon Cross. The lane had a most peculiar name. Penny something-or-other — "

"Penny Buckle Lane," Chris supplied.

"Lucky for you Jill Foster came along," Sam commented. "I take it you've been close friends of hers ever since?"

"Well — I don't know if you'd say we were close friends exactly — "

A faint frown troubled the usually serene brow of Hubert Morris. He found an ashtray and put it on the arm of Chris's chair before turning back to Sam.

"To be frank, Mr Harvey, after the accident happened we found ourselves in rather an embarrassing situation. We owed a great deal to Jill but, well damn it, the more we got to know the girl, the less we liked her."

"I think you're being a little unkind, Hubert," Chris interposed gently. "She's a strange creature, in more ways than one."

"I'm terribly unkind, Chris, I realise that. And I wouldn't talk to anyone else like this, but I want Mr Harvey to know the truth."

"Why don't you like her, Mr Morris?"

"Oh dear! I was afraid you'd ask that." Hubert glanced at Chris, perhaps seeking a silent go-ahead for what he was about to say. "I don't know why, but she always seems to be in some sort of trouble. Also — I hate to say this — but the people she mixes with, her so-called friends, they're absolutely awful. Dreadful people!"

"That's a slight exaggeration, darling."

From a nearby room came the sudden blast of a radio or cassette player with the volume turned up. The tune was one that had recently been top of the charts. Hubert had started for the door to tell his son to turn it off when the volume was lowered. Mother and father exchanged a smile of self-congratulation and Hubert relaxed.

"Have you met most of Jill's friends?" Sam asked.

"I wouldn't say most of them." It was Hubert who

answered the question. "But enough to be going on with!"

"Do you happen to know whether she's friendly with a man called Walter Randell?"

It was obvious that the name meant something to Hubert. He looked at Chris.

"I can't imagine anyone being friendly with Mr Randell," she said dryly.

"You know him?"

"I've met the gentleman — once. With my lawyer."

"Chris referred to Randell in an article she wrote and he threatened to sue her," Hubert explained. "Talking of Jill's friends, my pet aversion is a chap called Morgan. Phil Morgan. Have you come across him?"

"What does he look like?"

"Thick set, bearded. Bit of a rough diamond to look at. But oddly enough, he's got a very pleasant voice."

"What does he do?"

"Haven't a clue. But I'll wager whatever it is it's about as straight as Spaghetti Junction."

Chris laughed, as if she had never heard the expression before.

"Tell me," Sam went on, "has Jill ever introduced you to anyone called Hogarth?"

"Hogarth? No."

"Curiously enough," Chris said, "I've heard that name. Jill and I had lunch together about ten days ago and when we arrived at the restaurant one of the waiters said there'd been a telephone call for her from — I'm sure he said a Mr Hogarth."

"How did Jill react?"

"She just thanked him, that was all. I think she was a little surprised."

Sam nodded and looked meaningly at his watch. He

finished his drink and put the glass on top of one of the piles of books. Chris stubbed out her cigarette and stood up.

"Are you sure you won't have another drink?" Hubert invited, without great conviction.

"I'm quite sure, thank you."

They were being very polite but Sam was sure that they could hardly wait to discuss Jonathan's interpretation of Iago. The sudden blare of music had been a reminder from their son that he still existed and desired attention.

As Hubert opened the door and they moved out into the hall Chris said, "Mr Harvey, I don't know whether my husband mentioned it or not but I'd very much like to do an article on you and your book. It would be illustrated by Hubert. I'd let you see the article before it was published."

"It's very kind of you, I do appreciate it. But just at the moment — " Sam hesitated. The publicity could be very useful. "Let me think about it, Mrs Morris."

"Please do that," she said.

"Meanwhile, I'd be very grateful if you'd not mention my name — in connection with the book, I mean."

"If that's what you want."

Through the closed door of a room opening off the hall the beat of pop music was much more audible than from the sitting-room.

"Mrs Morris, forgive my asking," Sam said, "but I noticed that your son limps slightly. Is that a result of the accident?"

"Yes, it is."

"He'll always have a limp, I'm afraid," Hubert explained, for once avoiding his wife's eyes. "But it's a good deal better than it was."

"Has he met Jill Foster since the accident happened?"

"Jonathan?" Chris seemed genuinely astonished by the question.

"Yes."

"He's seen her. He saw her the evening she brought that awful Phil Morgan to dinner."

"I meant — does she take him out? Treat him to the cinema occasionally, that sort of thing?"

"No, she doesn't."

Chris shook her head emphatically. Hubert took his hand off the latch of the front door.

"Mr Harvey, please be frank with us. What is it you really want to know about Jonathan?"

Sam faced him directly and laid his card squarely on the table.

"I want to know if he was taken to Guildford one morning by Jill Foster?"

"Jonathan?" Hubert was shocked by the question. "Why, no!"

"Of course he wasn't!" Chris exclaimed. "Whatever gave you that idea?"

"You're sure?"

"Of course we're sure!" They were both staring at him, perplexed and a little angry. "Why should Jill want to take my son to Guildford?"

"You've answered my question, Mr Morris. Thank you."

Back at his flat Sam made himself a late cup of tea and put on a cassette of piano music. He had learnt from experience that this often induced a good mood for writing and he had resolved to put in two hours of work before going out to dinner at the Italian restaurant round the corner.

Even when he had sat down at his desk, however, he

found it hard to drive all the complexities of the Marius of Rye case out of his mind and concentrate on *Breakfast at the Zoo*. Rather like a tired person who cannot identify the exact moment of falling asleep he slipped unconsciously from the real world into the world of animals which had become so vivid to him.

The jangling of the telephone startled him into awareness. To his surprise darkness had fallen outside the window. The clock above the fireplace told him that over two hours had passed. He realised that he was hungry.

Irritated with the telephone for breaking into his mood he swivelled his chair round and reached for the instrument.

"Mr Harvey?"

"Speaking."

"This is Dr Majduli. St. Matthew's Hospital."

"Oh, hello, Doctor!" Sam said, immediately interested.

"Mr Harvey, I believe you asked me to get in touch with you if Miss Foster expressed a wish to see you again."

"Yes, I certainly did."

"Well, I gather from the Sister that Miss Foster wants to talk to you about something. The matter would appear to be urgent."

Sam was already pushing his chair back and standing up.

"Tell her I'll be there in about fifteen minutes! And thank you for ringing, Doctor."

He dropped the receiver on its stand and grabbed his coat from the back of the chair where he had thrown it. He picked up his wallet and keys from the desk and put them in his pocket. He made a quick tour of the flat, checking that all the windows were secured, especially his bedroom window which gave onto the fire-escape. Then he drew the curtains in the sitting-room. Turning out the lights he went through to the hall. He had put on his coat and opened the front door when he checked himself. He stood for a moment, hesitating, then he closed the door and went back into the sitting-room.

He had the number of the hospital in his head, but it took him several minutes and a good deal of verbal muscle before he eventually persuaded the switchboard to put him through to Dr Majduli's office.

"Doctor, this is Sam Harvey again."

"Yes, Mr Harvey," said the Indian, courteous as always. "What can I do for you?"

"I'm sorry to trouble you, but I wonder if you would be kind enough to give me some information before I leave for the hospital?"

"What is it you want to know?"

"Has Miss Foster received any visitors this evening?"

"Mr Brewster was here again today." Dr Majduli sounded amused. "He brought some more flowers."

"Did anyone else call?"

"Yes. Another gentleman called to see her about an hour ago."

"Did you see him?"

"Yes, I spoke to him. I told him not to stay too long because Miss Foster had been complaining of a headache. He was a stocky little man with a beard. I'm afraid I didn't catch his name."

"Thank you, Doctor."

Whereas before Sam's movements had been hurried and impulsive he was now slow and deliberate. He went into the kitchen, crouched down beside the fake dish-washer and opened the door. He operated the combination lock of the safe and took out the gun. He automatically checked that there were six rounds in the chamber and that the safety catch was applied. He closed the safe and

144

the dishwasher, stood up and slipped the gun into his coat pocket.

In the sitting-room he picked up the telephone again, dialled the number for a radio-cab and gave his address.

Moving faster now, he left the flat and hurried down to the street. It was a dry, clear night and above the roof-tops the stars were bravely trying to pierce the glow of London's lights. He went to the edge of the pavement and stood looking anxiously up and down the square.

All the space in the residents parking area was occupied. There were half a dozen cars on the single yellow line opposite. Thanks to the glow of lights in the streets at either end of the square he could see that they were all empty except one. The head of the driver was outlined against the rear window.

Sam began to walk quickly along the pavement. As he came level with the car the driver picked up a paper and tilted it so that the light from a street lamp illuminated it. The action also had the effect of hiding his face. Sam did not even glance in his direction. He was looking at his watch as he went past.

He was just level with the spot where the pavement had been taken up when a taxi swung into the square. He walked out into the middle of the road and held his hand up so that the driver could not pass. The taxi's brakes squealed as it stopped.

"Sorry, mate," the driver began, "I'm already — "

"I'm Harvey," Sam told him quietly. "It was me who rang you."

He twisted the handle of the door and added more audibly. "St Matthew's Hospital. As quickly as you can."

"Right, mate," the driver said. As the door banged the taxi jerked forward.

Before the taxi turned out of the square Sam leant

forward and spoke through the glass partition, which the driver had left ajar.

"Driver, I want you to turn left, go round the block and drop me near where you picked me up."

"I thought you said you wanted to go to St Matthew's—"

"I'm a police officer. Please do as I tell you. I'm in a hurry."

"Just my bleedin' luck," the driver muttered, but he put his foot down.

There was not a great deal of traffic in the main street and the taxi was lucky at the only set of traffic lights. But when the driver tried to take a short cut through a mews he ran into trouble. A Vauxhall, reversing out from one of the garages, had run into the side of a van. The two owners were getting out of their cars with that purposeful, deliberately slow manner which heralds a flare-up. The taxi driver played them a tune on his horn, but they took no notice.

When they got their notebooks out the driver turned round to see if he could reverse out of the jam, but another car had entered the mews and was blocking the way.

"Nothing I can do about this, guv."

Sam swore. The vital minutes were ticking away. Already the man in the car would have had time to go up to his flat and use skeleton keys in his door.

He took a note from his pocket and pushed it through the window at the driver.

"Here you are. It'll be quicker on foot."

The man was starting to complain when he saw that the note was a fiver.

"Thanks, mate," he shouted, as Sam ran past his window. "Best of luck to you."

Sam sprinted the length of the mews, which emerged into the square about three hundred yards from his house.

As he ran past the car which had been parked near the pavement works he saw that it was now empty. He slowed down to a walk as he approached the door of his house, to recover his breath, and then raced up the stairs three at a time.

The first thing he saw as he came onto the landing outside his own front door was that it was not quite closed. Someone had snicked the latch back and pushed it to without locking it — presumably to be sure of a quick getaway. He withdrew the revolver from his pocket and released the safety catch. Then he gently pushed the door open with his foot.

The interior of the flat was still dark, but in the light from the landing he saw something glittering on the carpet just inside the door. It was one half of a broken cuff-link. Remembering Bellamy's experience he checked himself as he was about to stoop and pick it up. That was a classic way of getting yourself coshed by a waiting assailant.

At that moment he heard a groan and a slithering sound from inside the flat. Holding the gun at the ready he reached a hand round the door-jamb and switched on the hall light. The small space was empty. He moved through it quickly and stopped again at the sitting-room doorway. There was a switch outside the door to turn the main light on. He pressed it down and as he did so he heard the groan again. There was no doubt now that it came from the kitchen.

Still wary of a trap Sam checked the space behind the sitting-room door before moving cautiously in, his gun at waist level ready to swing in any direction.

The room was empty, but he made a special point of checking the window curtains before moving to the kitchen door. The door was almost closed but he could see that the light was on.

Sam kicked the door open. It slammed back against the wall, allowing him a clear view of the whole room.

The man was lying in the middle of the floor, on his back. His eyes were wild with pain. His feet were slithering about on the floor. He had put both hands round the handle of the stiletto-style knife that was buried to the hilt in his chest, but he lacked either the strength or the resolution to pull it out.

One quick glance told Sam that he had only minutes to live unless he could be rushed into an intensive care unit. This was a case beyond first aid.

He went back to the sitting-room and picked up the telephone. As he dialled the three nines and waited for the disc to revolve with maddening slowness he had time to reflect that this was the third time he had called for an ambulance in the space of a few days.

When he had given his message and emphasised that every second counted he suddenly remembered the broken cuff-link.

He returned to the hall. The door was still wide open but the cuff-link had vanished.

8

In accordance with police policy Chief Superintendent Bert Sinclair was informing the press of any fresh developments in the Marius of Rye case, and relying on their discretion to keep certain aspects of the investigations out of the papers. He would have liked to hush up the latest incident in the flat of ex-Superintendent Sam Harvey, but an ambulance tearing through London with its siren wailing is not something you can keep secret, especially when half a dozen police cars converge with remarkable promptness on the house to which it has been called. A local free-lance journalist was very quickly on the scene and after that every crime editor in Fleet Street wanted a story.

Tired of answering calls from crime reporters avid for some exclusive angle Sam had dialled one digit and then left his telephone receiver off the stand. It was still that way at ten o'clock the next morning as he sat in the kitchen in his dressing-gown, drinking his last cup of coffee and smoking his first cigarette. A couple of newspapers lay on the table. His unopened mail lay on the hall table.

After getting to bed late he had woken up just in time to clean most of Phil Morgan's blood off the kitchen lino before Mrs Carr appeared. She had cooked him his breakfast while he bathed and shaved.

Now she was busy in the sitting-room, clearing up the mess created by ambulancemen and police officers tramping through the place.

He heard the doorbell ring but left Mrs Carr to answer it. He had briefed her that he was not receiving visitors unless their business was very urgent. To his annoyance he heard voices in the hall. They continued even when the front door had been shut.

A minute later Mrs Carr came into the kitchen, her blue rinse protected by the scarf she always wore over her head when dusting and hoovering.

"It's a young lady, sir," she whispered. "She says it's very important for her to see you —"

"Did you ask her name?"

"Yes. Miss Morris, I think she said."

It was evident that Mrs Carr took a more favourable view of Chris Morris than she had of Margaret Randell. More than once she had hinted to Sam that it was time he found a nice girl to marry and she had taken upon herself the responsibility of vetting his female visitors. "Miss" Morris obviously belonged to the highly suitable category.

"I suppose I'd better see her. Ask her to come in."

He finished his coffee and stubbed his cigarette out. Luckily he had put on a pair of slacks after shaving. He was tightening the belt of his dressing-gown as he entered the sitting-room.

Mrs Carr was just showing Chris in.

"I'm sorry to disturb you, Mr Harvey," said Chris, as Mrs Carr disappeared into the kitchen. "I tried to ring you but all I got was the engaged tone."

Sam gave a faint smile, but did not look towards the telephone. "What can I do for you, Mrs Morris?"

"I've just come from the office. We've had a report that a man broke into your flat last night and was attacked by someone. Is that true?"

"Yes, it is."

"What happened?" She opened her handbag and took out a notebook.

"It's difficult to say what happened. The police seem to think he disturbed someone who was already in the flat."

"I see. Who discovered the injured man?"

"I did. I'd been out and I returned unexpectedly. Morgan was on the floor, in the kitchen. He'd been stabbed."

She glanced up, her pencil poised above the page. "His name was Morgan?"

"Yes. Phil Morgan." Sam was watching her reaction. "I thought you knew that. He was the man we talked about. A friend of Jill Foster's."

She was obviously shaken by the news. "I didn't realise that — The report just said someone had broken into your flat. No name was mentioned. I never dreamt — What happened to Morgan?"

"He died on the way to hospital."

She sat down quickly on the settee, the notebook forgotten. "I find this quite incredible. What on earth was Phil Morgan doing in your flat?"

"I don't know."

"Haven't you any idea?"

"What's your guess? What do you think he was doing here?"

She was unsettled by him turning the question back on her. Her eyes darted round the room, avoiding him.

"I can't imagine, unless — Is this the first time your flat's been broken into?"

"No."

"What happened on the previous occasion?"

"Mrs Morris, forgive me," Sam said firmly, "but I have an appointment at eleven o'clock and there are a hundred and one things I've got to attend to this morning. Besides, there's really nothing more I can tell you at the moment. I'm sorry."

"I understand. And thank you for seeing me. Perhaps I could phone you later in the day, just in case — "

She stood up and put the notebook away. Sam replaced the receiver on the telephone stand.

"Yes, by all means do that."

She began to move towards the hall, but at the door she stopped. "Last night, after you left, Hubert and I were very puzzled. We just couldn't understand why you wanted to know whether our son, Jonathan, had ever visited Guildford."

"A boy called at my father's house, very early one morning, and delivered a parcel. He was about Jonathan's age and he had a slight limp."

"It wasn't Jonathan, I assure you."

When he had closed the door on her he stood looking at it. She had ostensibly come in search of an exclusive angle on the story. He was sure that her surprise at the mention of Phil Morgan had been genuine. But he wondered if the visit had been an excuse to repeat her denial that Jonathan had ever visited Guildford.

The telephone remained silent while he finished dressing, but he was still doing up his shoe laces when Bellamy arrived. When Sam joined him in the sitting-room the tall man was standing at the window taking deep breaths and straining his shoulders back.

"Sorry to have kept you, Bellamy."

Bellamy turned round and wagged his head from side to side to ease his neck muscles.

"That's all right. I was in the building making inquiries and I thought I'd like to have another word with you."

"Why not?" Sam said good-humouredly.

Bellamy frowned, half suspecting sarcasm or, worse still, condescension.

"I believe you said it was about nine-fifteen when you discovered Morgan?"

"Yes. I left here at five to nine. I know it was five to nine because I looked at my watch. I was away about fifteen minutes."

"Well, it's now been established that three people entered the block between the time you left and the time Morgan was murdered."

"Three people?"

"Yes. Two men and a woman. Obviously Morgan was one of the men, but according to our information he wasn't the first to arrive. The other man entered the block first. A tall man with glasses."

"A tall man with glasses?" Sam echoed sharply.

Bellamy shook his head.

"The description means precisely nothing. The glasses could have been part of a disguise. He probably wasn't even tall. Half the men in London seem to wear lifts these days."

Sam could not help glancing at Bellamy's enormous flat shoes.

"What about the woman?"

"She was the last to arrive. In fact, she must have entered the building about the same time as you. One of the residents — a Mrs Calthorpe — saw her. She described her as being 'a well-dressed woman in a hurry'."

"Do you think Mrs Calthorpe could identify her?"

"I doubt it very much. Why? Who are you thinking of?"

"I wasn't thinking of anyone in particular."

Bellamy stared distrustfully at Sam. "You know, the

thing that puzzles me, is why you didn't go to the hospital immediately the doctor telephoned."

"I don't know. It was just a hunch. Don't you get hunches, Bellamy?"

"Not if I can possibly avoid it. In my experience, they can be very misleading."

The telephone, which had been behaving with great discretion since Sam had replaced it, chose that moment to break its silence.

"Harvey speaking."

"Mr Harvey, this is Margaret Randell."

"Oh, hello, Margaret!"

Bellamy, affecting disinterest, picked up a newspaper and started to read it.

"I'm staying with some friends in Hampstead and I'd very much like to see you while I'm in Town. Is that possible?"

"Yes, of course. How long are you going to be in London?"

"I'm not sure. Two or three days."

"Well, why not drop in tomorrow morning for a drink? Let's say twelve o'clock?"

"Thank you. That's very sweet of you. I did call round last night but you were obviously out. Although, curiously enough, your front door was ajar."

"What time was that?"

"About nine o'clock, I suppose. Perhaps a little later. I rang the bell but there was no reply. I couldn't understand it."

"Did you see anyone, Margaret?"

"See anyone?"

"Whilst you were in the building?"

"No, I don't think so." She paused, trying to remember. "Now, wait a minute — just as I got to the bottom of the staircase a young man came down and went out of the building."

"What did this young man look like?"

"Oh dear! I'm awfully bad at this sort of thing. He was dark. Hair rather long. Quite honestly, I didn't really take much notice of him."

Bellamy had stopped pretending to read the paper and was now listening to Sam's end of the conversation with undisguised interest.

"I'm glad you telephoned, Margaret. I shall look forward to seeing you tomorrow. Goodbye."

Sam replaced the receiver and smiled at Bellamy.

"Well, that's answered one question. We know who the woman was."

By the time he had got rid of Bellamy Sam was running late for his appointment at his publishers. He gathered up the pages he had written during the past three days and pushed them into a document case. The telephone was ringing again as he left the flat. He shouted to Mrs Carr to answer it and ran down the stairs to the street. He had discovered from experience that the quickest and simplest way of getting to Long Acre was by underground. He was just turning towards South Kensington station when a Rolls-Royce pulled in to the kerb beside him. He glanced round, saw the liveried chauffeur in the driving seat and a familiar face smiling at him through the open rear window.

"Mr Harvey!"

"Why, hello, Mr Randell."

"This is a bit of luck. I was just going to call on you in the hope that we might have a chat."

"I'm sorry, but I'm in rather a hurry."

"Where are you off to? Can I offer you a lift?"

"No, I don't think so, thanks. I have an appointment in Long Acre."

"Long Acre? Jump in! I'll drop you."

"Are you sure?"

"Absolutely!" Randell assured him.

"Well, thank you. This is a great help."

Randell leant forward to open the door. Sam climbed in and sank back in the seat.

"Long Acre, Harold," Randell told his chauffeur, then pressed a button to close the glass partition.

Randell waited till the big car had purred out of the square and joined the traffic on the Brompton Road before he adjusted his spectacles and turned to Sam.

"I'm not by nature a curious man, Mr Harvey, but after our last meeting I must confess you made me curious."

"About what, exactly?"

"About your father and his relationship with my wife. In short, I wondered whether your friend — whoever he was — had got his facts right."

"Yes, he did. I spoke to Margaret about it and she explained what happened."

"Did she indeed? That's interesting. I saw Katie Mellowfield last night and she told me her version of what happened. I wonder if it's the same as Margaret's?"

"You can very easily find out," Sam told him.

"How?"

"Do what I did, Mr Randell. Ask your wife."

"I'd much prefer to ask you, Mr Harvey. What did Margaret tell you?"

"She said that going to the Leopard Club and having dinner with my father was entirely her idea. She simply wanted to repay my father for the kindness he'd shown her."

156

Randell appeared somewhat discomfited by this statement. "That's precisely what Katie Mellowfield told me," he said, as if it was an admission.

"Well, there you are."

"Fancy Margaret telling you the truth! You must have a very salutary effect on my wife, Mr Harvey." The interior of the car was warm but he leant forward to turn the heating even higher. "Tell me, this friend of yours — was it by any chance a colleague, Superintendent Bellamy?"

"Yes, it was."

"I thought so. Katie Mellowfield said he'd been making inquiries."

"About my father?"

"Not only about your father. About me too, curiously enough. Although why he should be interested in me, I can't imagine."

"You're a very wealthy man, Mr Randell."

"Is that a crime?" He turned to give Sam an innocent smile.

"No. But you appear to make a great deal of money very easily."

"I am that rarest of species, a gambler who makes it pay. But it's not by any means an easy way to make a living. So if by any chance you're thinking of taking it up, Mr Harvey, my advice is, don't."

"The thought hadn't entered my head. And my heart bleeds for you, Mr Randell."

"I'm delighted to hear it. I shall be even more delighted when your friend, Bellamy, feels the same way."

Harold was an expert chauffeur. Sam had done the course at the police driving school but he had to admire the way the man whisked the big car through the mid-morning traffic. He knew his London as well as any taxi driver and sneaked through side streets to deposit Sam outside the Long Acre offices of Scofield and Ray a minute before the time of his appointment.

"Thank you for the lift, it's been a great help."

"My pleasure." Randell indicated the sign on the wall beside the door. "Your publishers, I take it?"

"Er — yes," Sam admitted, taken aback by the other's inspired guess.

"Are you writing another book, Mr Harvey?"

"Yes, as a matter of fact, I am."

"Don't look so surprised," Randell said with a chuckle. "You've been investigating me, so I thought I'd investigate you."

Sam spent an hour and a half in Scofield's office ironing out some of the problems which he was having with his draft for the second book. Afterwards they lunched at a wine bar in the former Covent Garden market. By the time they had finished Scofield had convinced Sam that he must not tear up the pages he had already written. Strangely enough, Scofield commented, the stress of working against the background of the Marius of Rye affair had tightened up his style, making him write even better than before.

He decided that before going home to start on a new chapter he would call in on Bert Sinclair at Scotland Yard. He wanted to explain that since giving his word he had not sought involvement with the investigation. He had not gone out in search of information. The case kept coming in search of him. He had not sought the meeting with Walter Randell or Chris Morris, nor gone out of his way to invite Margaret to his flat. And it was hardly his fault if Bellamy, Jill Foster and Phil Morgan had all been attacked at his home. The place seemed to exercise a mysterious attraction for everyone connected with the mystery of his parents' murder.

When he reached Sinclair's office he found that Bellamy had just beaten him to it. The Chief Superintendent waved him to a chair.

"We shan't be a moment, Sam. I just want to straighten some things out with Bellamy."

Sam sat down and picked up a copy of the *Daily Telegraph*. Bert had kept Bellamy standing. He picked up a sheet of A4 paper covered with close typewritten lines.

"It's this memo of yours, Bellamy. I may be dense, but frankly I don't understand a word of it."

"It's about Corby, sir. The camera shop. You remember Corby?"

"Of course I remember Corby!" As always Bert was irritated by Bellamy's primness. "The man who brought us the film."

"That's right."

Bert tapped the memo sheet with the back of his hand. "But what's all this about a boat and Poole Harbour?"

"Mr Corby has two secondhand furniture shops. One in Weybridge, the other in Addlestone." Bellamy glanced at Sam to see if he was listening. "I've had the dubious pleasure of visiting both."

"Well?"

"Frankly, if he makes a hundred pounds a week out of both of them I shall be very, very surprised."

"So?"

"So how come Mr Corby owns a yacht?"

"Owns a yacht?"

Sam smiled into his newspaper. So often he had heard these two fence with each other like this. Bellamy loved to hide cards up his sleeve so that he could produce them when he had goaded Bert into angry impatience.

"Yes. It's in Poole Harbour. It's called 'Easy Living'. And according to a friend of mine who understands boats it must have cost at least a hundred thousand."

"Are you sure the yacht belongs to Corby?"

"Quite sure. I've checked and double checked."

"Well, if what you say is true there's something damn funny about this! Corby, a secondhand furniture dealer, owns a yacht worth over a hundred thousand — "

"And Jason Harvey," Bellamy added, "a retired insurance salesman, leaves an estate worth half a million."

"It just doesn't add up. What's this about the camera shop and someone called Naylor?"

"Arthur Naylor. He's the chap who runs Surrey Snapshots. I had another session with Naylor and — well, in the end he admitted that he hardly knew Corby. He said Corby paid him five hundred pounds just to confirm his story."

Bert dropped the memo sheet, stood up and came round his desk.

"Let's get this straight. What you're saying is, the film was processed privately and Corby knew perfectly well what was on it, right from the start."

"That's exactly what I'm saying. Corby may even have taken the film."

"But why bring it here? What was the point?"

"Well, sir, my theory — which I've included at the end of my memo — is that — "

Bellamy was ready to move into top gear when the door opened. A studious-looking man in civilian clothes appeared. He had an abnormally high forehead, crowned with wiry, tousled hair and wore a pair of semi-circular steel-rimmed glasses. When not engaged in close work he peered over the top of these with puckered eyes. Startled by the sight of the towering Bellamy he halted on the threshold. Sam recognised the notebook in his hand as the one George Adams had given him.

"Oh, I'm sorry, sir. I beg your pardon."

"Come in, Osgood." Bert waved him in good-humouredly. "Come along in."

Osgood blinked nervously at Sam.

"I can drop in later, sir, if you'd rather."

"No, no, that's all right." Bert went and shut the door behind Osgood. He put a protective arm round him and steered him into the room. "How are you making out with Jason Harvey's notebook? Any progress?"

"It's not easy but we'll get there in the end. Right now, I'd like some information, sir."

"Go ahead. What is it you want to know?"

Osgood hesitated, as if he was about to ask for the moon.

"If Jason Harvey had a car I'd like to know the registration number."

"That's no problem."

"And the van — with Marius of Rye on it."

Bert lifted his eyebrows at Bellamy.

"The van was stolen," Bellamy said. "It had false number plates."

"I know the plates were false. But what was the registration number?"

Bert went back behind his desk and began to hunt through the papers lying on it.

"I'll tell you in a minute. I've got it here somewhere. Now where the devil did I put it?" He triumphantly pounced on a typewritten sheet. "Ah, here we are!"

"Is it GYT 842N?" Osgood asked quickly, anxious to make a guess before Bert told him.

Bert looked up at him. "No."

Osgood was disappointed. He studied the notebook again.

"NPE 296F?" he tried, and his mouth stayed open as he peered at Bert over his spectacles.

"No." Bert shook his head, entering into the spirit of Osgood's little game. He waited a second then said, "It's JKN 405N."

"Oh." Osgood scratched the top of his head, crestfallen. "Oh, dear."

"Problems?" Bert suggested helpfully.

"Not really." The codes and ciphers expert seemed far away as he scrutinised the notebook and a sheet he had inserted between the pages. "I'm on the right track, I'm sure." Then he shook his head, flashed a smile at Bert and turned on his heel. As he dived towards the door he muttered, "Back to the drawing-board, Osgood."

His conversation with Scofield had given Sam a shot in the arm. He had told Sinclair and Bellamy all he knew and was more than happy now to let them get on with the case. Scofield wanted to have *Breakfast at the Zoo* as quickly as possible so that they could all cash in on the immediate success of his first book. Sam asked for nothing better than to be left in peace to finish the final chapters.

He had written fifteen hundred words at least when a sense of cold and hunger broke his concentration. He pushed his chair back, stretched and stood up. He went to the wall and turned on the electric convector-heater, drew the curtains across the dark window, found a cigarette and lit it.

From the flat above came the clack of the woman walking about in high heels. He wished she and her flat-mate would lay a carpet on their sitting-room floor. The cassette he had put on when he started working had finished long ago. Now the speakers were emitting a faint background hiss, like gas gently escaping. The sound reminded him of his boyhood in Pennymore and the fire in his cosy little room. So often he had taken refuge there when Jason Harvey had made him feel a shade unwanted. He had tried so hard to like his step-father but he had never been able to overcome his instinctive distrust of him. Now he knew that he had been right.

He sat down again, but the mood had gone. He wrote a few lines then scrumpled the sheet up and flung it into the waste-paper basket. He was starting on a fresh sheet when the telephone rang.

He looked at it, wondering whether to answer it or not. Then, with a resigned shrug, he picked up the receiver. Immediately he heard the intermittent tone which told him that the call was coming from a payphone.

"Harvey?" demanded a breathless voice.

"Yes. Who is that?"

"This is Bellamy. Listen, Harvey! When the doorbell rings, don't answer it!"

"What are you talking about — ?"

"Did you hear what I said?"

"Yes, I heard. But why on earth — ?"

"Do as I say!" Bellamy almost shouted. "Keep away from the door! Don't open it to anyone!"

The phone was slammed down. Sam replaced his more quietly. He sat thinking. It was not at all like Bellamy to panic.

All hope of getting on with his story had now vanished. He pushed his chair back and went out to the hall. Both locks were properly secured. He shot the heavy bolt he had fitted since the intrusion of Phil Morgan. In the kitchen he opened the fridge, found a bottle of milk and poured half a pint into a saucepan to heat. He found the tin of Ovaltine and a packet of chocolate digestive biscuits in the cupboard where Mrs Carr had tidied them. As he waited for the milk to come to the boil he stood leaning against the wall, eating the biscuits.

The woman upstairs had ceased her perambulations and turned on her TV for the nine o'clock news. The bass tones of the announcer's voice penetrated the floor-boards. Through the kitchen window he could see across the skimpy garden to the backs of the houses in the next street. Feeling conspicuous under the brilliant neon light he leant forward and pulled the string that closed the venetian blinds.

What on earth was Bellamy up to now? It was irritating of the man not to give him a bit more information to go on. There was no way of telling whether the call had been made from near or far. Odd chap, Bellamy. He had never found out why his phone number had been among those listed on the book of matches in Jill Foster's handbag.

A sudden hiss and the smell of burning warned him that he'd allowed the milk to boil over. He whipped it quickly off the ring, knocking a spoon onto the floor. As he stooped the doorbell started to ring.

He picked the spoon up and replaced it beside the cup. He listened to the bell ringing, staring through the open door to the sitting-room. After half a minute or so the bell stopped.

Sam wiped the top of the hot-plate with a damp cloth. He poured the milk on top of the spoonful of Ovaltine he had put in the cup, stirring as he did so.

The bell started ringing again — short, urgent peals this time instead of the long insistent ones.

He set the cup down, walked slowly through the sitting-room and into the hall. He stood there, looking at the

164

closed door. The bell was near his ear now and it sounded very loud.

Then it stopped. The door shook under the frantic beating of clenched fists. He thought he heard a sob of despair.

He stood back against the wall and called out, "Who's there?"

"It's Jill," a desperate voice answered. "Jill Foster. Please — please let me in."

9

"Looks to me as if you could both use a drink."

Sam had locked and bolted the front door before following his two visitors into the sitting-room. Peter Brewster was shaken and a little ashamed of himself. He had sent Jill on up to Sam's flat ahead of him while he parked and locked the car and then in his hurry had jammed the key in the lock.

"I'm terribly sorry about that, Jill," he said, still apologising. "I really am."

"It's all right. I just panicked, finding myself alone out there on the landing, and no one answering the bell."

She was white and strained and Sam thought the pupils of her eyes were unnaturally large. She went across to the sofa and sank down.

"I don't think she'd better have a drink, Mr Harvey," Peter said. "The doctor gave her an injection just before we left the hospital. But I could do with a whisky myself if you've got one."

Sam nodded and went to the drinks table. He took his time pouring Peter Brewster's whisky. The couple needed a few moments to settle down. They were both as nervous as field-mice.

Peter took his glass and took an appreciative swallow. He sat down on the arm of the sofa close to Jill.

"We had a long talk this evening and I finally persuaded Jill to come here and tell you the truth. She's now prepared to tell you exactly what happened to your parents after she picked them up at Heathrow."

Sam moved round so that he could see Jill's face. She hesitated, then began to talk in an urgent, breathless voice.

"Some time ago, shortly after I'd been arrested for shop-lifting, I did another very stupid thing. I thought I'd got away with it. I felt sure no one knew about it. Then one morning a man I'd never met, or even heard of, started blackmailing me."

"He made Jill work for him," Peter put in, his hand on her shoulder. "Deliver messages. Contact certain people."

"When did you first meet this man?"

She shook her head. "I haven't met him. Not that I know of. He simply gives me instructions over the phone."

"Is it always the same man?"

"Yes."

"You're sure?"

"I'm quite sure. It's the same voice and he invariably uses the same name. Hogarth."

"But that's what you called my father when you picked him up at Waterloo."

"Yes, I know."

Sam rubbed the inside of his finger with his thumb.

"Was my father working for Hogarth?"

She glanced up at Peter before answering. He gave her a nod of encouragement.

"Yes, he was. When I addressed your father as Hogarth he knew immediately that I had a message for him. I gave it to him on the way to the airport."

"What was the message?" Sam asked quietly.

"I told him that Hogarth would be waiting for him at Heathrow — that something important had arisen and that the trip to Australia had to be postponed."

Sam's face betrayed no emotion. He seemed as detached as if this case was simply a routine enquiry.

167

"What was my father mixed up in?"

Again she hesitated before answering. "Drugs."

"Drugs? Hard or soft?"

"I've never understood the difference, but most of the cannabis resin destined for the United States used to be routed through Amsterdam. Well — Hogarth and your father changed all that. It's now brought to this country and despatched from here."

"As I understand it," Peter added, "that's what your father was concerned with the day he was killed."

"After I picked them up at the airport I took them to a house in Kent — "

"In Kent?" Sam broke in, puzzled. "Not Oxfordshire?"

"No, in Kent. Near Gravesend. That's where your father collected the van. His destination was Dover. Unfortunately, he never got that far."

"Why Dover?"

Her distress was evident. Sam could not tell whether she was suffering from remorse or the effects of the injection she had been given. Peter Brewster gave her an encouraging pat and answered for her.

"An agent of Hogarth's, a man called Marius, had arrived from the Continent with a supply of cannabis resin. He was a cautious bastard and flatly refused to deal with anyone other than your father. Not only that — he knew that the customs men were on the alert. So he insisted that your father picked him up in a van bearing the name Marius of Rye. He even supplied Hogarth with a photograph of the van. It was a name he'd invented for the occasion and which no-one else knew about. Had your father arrived in any other vehicle, Marius wouldn't have contacted him."

"Is this true, Jill?"

"Yes, I'm afraid it is."

"You're very well informed, Mr Brewster."

"I'm merely repeating what Jill has already told me."

"What else has she told you?"

Peter stole a quick look at Sam's face trying to guess what the sharpness in his voice meant.

"Larry Voss and Phil Morgan also worked for Hogarth, but there was a quarrel and they tried to take over from him."

"So Hogarth killed Voss," Jill said.

"But weren't you a friend of Phil Morgan's?"

"I helped him on one or two occasions," she admitted. "But for one reason and one reason only. I was determined to find out who Hogarth was. I felt that once I knew who was blackmailing me I'd be in a much stronger position."

"To do what?" Sam asked with slight scepticism.

"Well — to break away from him, of course."

"And did you find out his identity?"

"No, I didn't, but about a month ago I met a friend of mine called Chris Morris in the "Prince Hal". While we were there Larry Voss came in. He was joined by a man called Walter Randell. After they left a colleague of yours, Superintendent Bellamy, arrived." She glanced nervously at Sam, then went on rather lamely. "I don't know why, it's difficult to explain, but — I had the impression that one of them was Hogarth. That's why I was curious about them. Why I made a note of their phone numbers."

"Mr Harvey, whichever way you look at it," Peter put in quickly, "Jill's in a difficult situation. Right from the start Hogarth has thrown suspicion on her. You remember the film Corby showed you. Now, supposing something happens to her, supposing her death is made to look like suicide — what will your friends at the Yard think?"

"I don't know," Sam said innocently. "What will they think?"

"They'll think that Hogarth doesn't exist, won't they? They'll think that Jill invented him."

"Then what do you suggest, Mr Brewster?"

"I think Jill ought to go into hiding. Now, before it's too late."

Sam did not smile at the suggestion, melodramatic though it sounded. He looked seriously from Jill to Peter.

"I think you told me that you have a cottage in the country."

"In Suffolk."

"Do many people know about it?"

"Very few."

"Then my advice is — take Jill there."

Peter nodded. It was obvious that Sam had endorsed the idea he had already put to Jill. She reached up to take his hand.

"How long should I have to stay?"

"Until Mr Brewster hears from me. But I don't think either of you should go home first. Go to the cottage now without delay."

Peter squeezed Jill's hand and stood up. He finished his whisky and gave Sam a grateful smile.

"I'll fetch the car. I had to park it some way up the street. I'll sound the horn when I'm ready."

Sam nodded. "I'll bring her down."

Peter went out to the hall. Sam had not shot the bolt again and the key was still in the mortice lock. He was just turning it when the doorbell rang. Unaware of Bellamy's warning message he assumed that this was another friend of Sam's. He opened the door.

The man standing outside was large, dark-jowled and arrogantly confident. He was smiling broadly. In his right hand was a black automatic. He pushed it forward a few inches.

"Mr Harvey, you have a visitor."

Peter Brewster kept his head. He stared at the gun for a few minutes, then backed away from the door.

The visitor followed him in, gun levelled steadily, and kicked the door shut.

"Turn around," he commanded in a strong East End accent. "Into the lounge. No tricks."

Peter turned round as commanded. He could see into the sitting-room. The settee was empty. He walked through the door, fast enough to make the visitor shamble quickly after him. Behind him he heard a quick movement, the sound of bone on bone, the clatter of the automatic falling to the floor and the man's gasp of pain and astonishment. By the time he had turned round the gun was in Sam's hand. The intruder was nursing a paralysed wrist. Jill, terrified, was standing like a statue behind the door.

"A case of mistaken identity," Sam said calmly. "I'm Harvey."

The man blinked from one to the other, too astonished and furious with himself to even curse.

"Take Jill and get out of here," Sam told Peter. "Remember what I said."

"You don't think I'll use this, do you?"

Sam was sitting on an upright chair, facing his uninvited guest from a safe distance. The other was on the sofa. Outside in the street a car started up and accelerated rapidly away.

"I'm damn sure you won't," the other said with insolent confidence.

"Then why don't you just get up and walk out, Mr Wilde?"

The visitor's jaw dropped.

"You know who I am then?"

"I recognised you right away. You're Tom Wilde. It's a very good hair piece you're wearing. But you really should do something about that nose. When did they let you out, Tom? Why did you come here? Who sent you?"

Wilde shifted nervously, his arrogance gone.

"I'm not talking. It's not on. No way — "

"I think it is on, Tom. Believe me, if you don't tell me what happened I shall have no alternative but to use this." Sam raised the gun an inch. "In self defence."

"What do you mean — self defence?"

"By the time my colleagues get here this room will be a shambles. I'm sure your friend Bellamy — who, incidentally, warned me of your visit — will very quickly weigh up the situation. He can be very perceptive, can Superintendent Bellamy."

Bellamy's methods of interrogation had earned him an enviable reputation in London's underworld. Wilde ran a finger round the inside of his collar.

"What do you want to know?"

"Who sent you?"

"A man called Corby. He paid me five hundred quid. I had to get certain information out of you."

Like most of his type, once Wilde had decided that it was in his best interest to sing he had no compunction in betraying his employer.

"About what?"

"About a notebook belonging to your father."

"Go on."

"Corby and his friends want that notebook and they seem to think you've got it. If you haven't got it, then they're pretty sure you know where it is."

"Where did you meet this man Corby?"

Wilde's voice was hoarse. Without putting his hand over his mouth he gave vent to a rasping cough.

"In a wine bar."

"Was Corby alone when you met him?"

"Look, do you think I could have a drink before we go any further with this?"

Sam ignored the request. "Was Corby alone when you met him?"

"Yes, he was alone, but after we'd been talking for about ten or fifteen minutes he was called to the phone."

"Who was the call from, do you know?"

"He was in a box," Wilde answered sullenly. "I couldn't hear what he was saying."

"I didn't ask you that."

"It might have been from someone called Hobart."

"Was the name Hogarth?"

"Yes, that's right," Wilde grinned with fake surprise. "Hogarth. It was after he'd spoken to Hogarth that he agreed to pay me the five hundred."

By the time Sam reached Addlestone most of the inhabitants had gone to bed. Only a few lights showed behind the windows of the side street where he parked his car. As he got out he saw two dark figures at the corner watching him. They were a couple of young motor-cyclists in black leathers. Their machines had been propped on the side-stands and their helmets placed on the seats. Still and silent they watched Sam lock the Porsche. He did not take any notice of them, but walked off down the street, checking the numbers on the houses.

He passed one pub. It had been closed for half an hour and only two cars remained in the park. A couple slid further down into their seats as he passed. There were still a few pedestrians about, dim figures in the poorly-lit street. He had gone a hundred yards when he became aware that someone was following behind him. He veered into the recessed doorway of a shop and took his time over lighting a cigarette. A man with coat-collar turned up slouched past with his hands in his pockets. After a moment Sam moved on.

There was no number above Corby's shop. A sign across the top of the window read, "Antiques. Second-hand furniture bought and sold." From what he could see through the window there was more junk than antiques. The surrounds of the windows badly needed repainting and it was a long time since the glass had been cleaned.

There was light behind the windows above the shop, over which badly-fitting curtains had been drawn. At the side of the shop was a dark, narrow alley. Sam took the torch from the left-hand pocket of his coat and shone it down the alley. Twenty feet along there was a doorway on the same side as the shop. He checked that the street was empty before moving in. A small rectangle glowed beside a bell-push and the speaker of an entry-phone. It bore no name. Sam pressed the button. He thought he faintly heard a buzzer somewhere above but there was no answer.

He pressed the button again. Suddenly the loudspeaker crackled in his ear. Corby's voice was only just recognisable.

"Who is that?"

"That you, Corby?" Sam said, making his voice hoarse and adopting his best Cockney accent.

"Yes. Who's that?"

"It's Tom. Tom Wilde. Count yourself lucky. I've got what you wanted."

There was a pause before Corby answered.

"Come along up."

There came a buzz as the automatic lock was released. The door sprang open a few inches. Sam pushed his way in, found himself in a small hall furnished only by a floor mat and a Victorian hat and umbrella stand. A steep, narrow flight of stairs led up to a landing. It was lit by a low-watt bulb.

Sam's hand was on the butt of the revolver in his right coat pocket as he carefully mounted the creaking stairs. The door leading off the landing had a round handle and no Yale lock. A strip of light showed under it. There was silence from the other side.

Sam withdrew the automatic from his pocket. In one movement he twisted the handle of the door and thrust it open with his right leg. It went crashing back against the wall behind. Light flooded out.

Slowly Sam straightened up from his half-crouched position. He let his gun-hand drop.

Leo Corby was standing in the middle of the room, facing the door as he waited for his visitor. On either side of him were two uniformed policemen. Corby's right wrist was handcuffed to one of them. A little to one side of the group stood a tall figure in plain clothes. He was holding a revolver identical to the one in Sam's hand.

"Harvey!" he exclaimed, taken utterly by surprise. "What the devil — "

"Hello, Bellamy," Sam said.

When Corby had been taken away by the two uniformed men Bellamy generously waved Sam to a button-upholstered Victorian chair and sat himself down in a high wing-backed chair covered with faded tapestry. Corby's Addlestone pied-à-terre consisted of only one room. It was furnished with spin-off from his spurious antique business, including a massive brass bedstead. The best piece in the room was a magnificent partners' desk. On it, incongruously, was one of the most modern telephone sets with a recording device attached. Equally out of place was a large TV set with a video-recorder. Amongst the piles of

175

leather-bound volumes at one side of the room was a case of champagne, which had been ripped open. Corby must have been celebrating something for an empty bottle stood on his chest of drawers.

"As soon as I realised what Wilde was up to I telephoned you," Bellamy explained, in answer to Sam's question. "And you were lucky, Harvey. Extremely lucky, in my opinion. If Peter Brewster hadn't been with you, my bet is you wouldn't be here now."

"How did you know about Wilde?"

"I had a man tailing Corby." Bellamy had adopted his habitual air of self-congratulation, building up his ego. "He knew Corby had contacted Wilde and he heard a rumour to the effect that he intended to drop in on you. I checked with an informant of mine and he confirmed the story."

"Well — thank you for the warning, Bellamy. I'll do the same for you sometime."

"I hope it won't be necessary."

Sam looked at him inquiringly as the buzzer from the entry-phone sounded.

"That'll be Sinclair," Bellamy said. "I asked him to get out here as quickly as he could."

The Chief Superintendent had been anticipating an early night in bed facing the TV set which he kept in his bedroom. He was ready to tear a strip off Bellamy for dragging him out to Addlestone at midnight but when he saw Sam he calmed down. Prowling round the room, picking up snuff-boxes, cigarette cases, inlaid boxes, he listened while Bellamy put him in the picture about Corby's arrest and Sam told him about the visitation from Tom Wilde.

"Where is he now?"

"In the cells at Brompton Square."

"Well, we now know they were after the notebook belonging to your father."

"Has Osgood cracked it yet?" Sam asked Bert.

"He delivered his report this evening," Bellamy said. "I sent it down to you, sir, with a memo."

Bert smiled and gave Sam a private wink.

"According to Osgood, the book simply contains three numbers. Three car registration numbers."

"Nothing else?"

"Nothing of importance. Unless Osgood's got it all wrong, which I don't think he has. He says the other details are irrelevant, just a cover-up for the car numbers."

"Have you located the cars?"

"Give us a chance, Sam! Osgood's only just come up with this."

"What are the numbers?"

Bert sat down in the button-upholstered chair and produced his notebook. He licked a finger and rapidly flicked over a score of pages. "Here we are. MKO 623P, THK 964N and SUX 876M?"

"SUX 876M?" Sam repeated.

"Yes. Do you know that number?"

"Yes, I do. At least, I've seen it."

"Where?"

"On a photograph belonging to Larry Voss." Bert looked puzzled. Sam went on, "The night Larry Voss was murdered I found two photographs in his suitcase. One was a photograph of a boat — a yacht called 'Easy Living'."

"We know about 'Easy Living'," Bellamy told Sam. "It's owned by our friend Corby. The Dorset CID took a look at it yesterday afternoon. They discovered cannabis resin worth the best part of a quarter of a million."

Sam tried to hide his resentment at not being given this important piece of information.

"Tell us about the other photograph, Sam," Bert suggested.

"It was a photograph of a car my father owned. A Marina. SUX 876M. He told me he'd sold it three months ago."

"Do you know who he sold it to?"

"No, I don't. I remember asking him at the time but he never got around to telling me."

"Why should Larry Voss have a photograph of your father's car?"

"I can only think of one reason. He wanted to make sure he'd recognise the car when he saw it."

"I don't follow you," Bellamy put down the empty champagne bottle he had been sniffing. Sam was not sure whether the look of disapproval was directed at the bottle or at him.

"Neither do I," Bert said. "What's on your mind, Sam?"

"Just before Tom Wilde turned up I had a visit from Jill Foster. She'd been persuaded by her boyfriend Peter Brewster that her best interests would be served if she came clean with me."

Bellamy was ready to take offence at anything which suggested that Sam was still interfering in the case and poaching on his territory, but his manner changed when he realised how surprised Sam had been by Jill's visit.

"So, where does that leave us?"

"I have a theory, Bert. It's only a theory, mind — "

"Let's hear it."

Bert had been eyeing the case of champagne for some time. Now, as Sam talked, he went across to it, picked out a bottle and started examining the label.

"Although my father worked for Hogarth, I have a feeling that he was, well, playing ducks and drakes with him. It's my bet that when you find the three cars — the cars mentioned in my father's notebook — you'll also find a supply of cannabis resin."

"Hidden in the cars?"

"Yes."

Bert came to a decision. He gave Sam a quick grin and began to peel the foil off the top of the bottle.

"Your father helped himself to a consignment of cannabis originally intended for Hogarth?"

"Right. Voss suspected what my father was up to. That's why he had a photograph of one of the cars and why he and Morgan searched the flat. Like Hogarth, they thought I had the notebook."

"How many people know that you've consulted us? That we've got this notebook?"

"You, me, Bellamy and Osgood."

"No-one else?"

"No-one else so far as I'm concerned. I certainly haven't mentioned it to anyone."

Bert was pushing the cork upwards with his thumbs, the pressure from inside helping him. Bellamy affected not to notice.

"Who is Hogarth? Have you any idea?"

"I have an idea, Bellamy. I also have a plan for flushing him out — or her. But whether you and Bert would be prepared to go along with it is another matter."

The cork came out with a sharp report. Bert tilted the bottle at an angle of forty-five degrees to control the effervescence.

"Fetch that set of cut glasses, Bellamy," Bert invited. "Let's sample this stuff while we listen to Sam's plan."

10

"Hello, Margaret! Do come in."

"Am I too early for you?"

"Not a bit," Sam assured his visitor warmly. "I'm delighted to see you."

As they entered the sitting-room Sam indicated the phone. "Will you excuse me if I just finish this telephone call?"

Margaret nodded and unfastened the coat she was wearing. "Yes, of course. I'm in no hurry." Sam picked up the receiver.

"Sorry about that, George . . . Well, look here — if you think it's so important could you bring it up? . . . Tonight? . . . Yes, I shall be here all evening . . . No, that's fine. I'll look forward to seeing you . . . What do you think is in the envelope?"

He turned to smile encouragingly at Margaret who had sat down and was arranging her skirt.

"A what? . . . I can't remember my father saying anything about a notebook — it can't be very important . . . Anyway, bring it along and we'll take a look at it . . . Yes, I will . . . See you tonight, George. Thanks for ringing."

He replaced the phone and made a wry face. "Sorry about that, Margaret. It was George Adams, my father's solicitor. I believe you met him. Nice chap but gets terribly bogged down. Now, can I offer you a drink?"

As Margaret hesitated.

"I'm going to have a very large sherry," Sam said encouragingly, moving to the drinks table. "What would you like?"

"May I have a very small sherry?"

"But of course." Sam took the stopper from the decanter and began to fill two schooners. "I expect you read about what happened. The night you came here and couldn't get any reply."

"Yes, I read about it, but I must admit I was very confused. What did happen?"

"While I was out, a stranger — a man called Morgan — broke into my flat and was murdered. What he was doing here, who murdered him, or why he was murdered, I just don't know." He handed her a glass. "You said on the phone that the door was open when you arrived here?"

"It was slightly ajar. I rang the bell, I rang it several times, but nothing happened. In the end I came to the conclusion that you'd slipped out for a few minutes — probably into one of the other flats."

"What time would that be?"

"About nine o'clock."

"And that's when you saw the young man, the man you mentioned?"

Sam was standing looking down at her, sipping his sherry.

"Not when I was leaving. I saw him when I arrived, just as I got to the bottom of the stairs. But as I said I really didn't pay much attention to him. The reason I wanted to see you was because I have the feeling that — "

She broke off and fiddled uneasily with the pearls at her throat.

"What is it, Margaret?"

"I think Pennymore has been searched."

"Searched?"

"Yes. The last time I was in your parents' house the day before yesterday, I had the impression that someone else had been there ahead of me."

"I wonder." Sam nodded thoughtfully, obviously in- clined to take her impression seriously. "I wonder if you're right?"

"It may have been just my imagination, but somehow I don't think it was. I really don't — "

Sam switched on his infectious grin and dismissed such sombre matters. He drew up a chair close to her.

"Well, anyway, it's nice to see you again, Margaret. Thank you for coming. Skol!"

She raised her glass on a level with his, then examined it with one of those smiles which conveyed the idea that a girlish spirit still survived within that mature breast.

"Is this what you call a very small sherry?"

Margaret Randell stayed on for longer than Sam had intended, flirting with him in the uncommitted way that middle-aged women have with younger men. In the end he got rid of her by agreeing to have dinner with her at the Leopard Club.

When she had left he just had time to get out the sketches which she had brought him in the Marius of Rye carrier bag on an earlier visit. He took them from the manilla envelope and left them where his next visitor could not fail to see them.

Hubert Morris arrived at ten to one, only five minutes after the time Sam had given him. He seemed a little nervous as he came into the sitting-room.

"I'm on the phone at the moment," Sam apologised. "Won't keep you long. Make yourself at home."

He picked up the phone lying on the desk.

"Sorry, George! A friend of mine has just arrived . . . What were you saying? . . . Yes. I'll be here all evening . . . Ten o'clock? . . . That's fine . . . I can hardly think the notebook you've got is of any importance, or my father would have mentioned it to me . . . Anyway, bring it along . . . Yes, of course I will. 'Bye George! See you tonight."

He put the phone down with a sigh and turned to his guest.

"George Adams, my father's lawyer. Awfully nice chap, but a terrible worrier. Do sit down, Mr Morris."

Hubert did not sit down. He was still staring at the sketches.

"Did you do these?"

"What? Oh, those sketches?" Sam gathered them up and thrust them back in the envelope. "Good heavens, no!"

"Well, whoever did them must be an admirer of mine."

"Why do you say that?"

"Because they're a copy of my work, my dear chap. That's why! And not a bad copy either. I'm flattered. You usually have to die before this sort of thing happens to you." Hubert finally accepted the invitation to sit down. "I was quite excited when I got your message. I gather it's to do with your new book?"

"I saw Henry Scofield the other day. When I told him my new book was well on its way he asked me to get in touch with you. He wants you to start work on the illustrations straight away."

"Before you've finished the book?"

"Yes, I thought it wouldn't do any harm if we had a little chat. At least it'll stop the old boy from badgering you."

"I agree. It's a good idea."

"But first, let me get you a drink. What would you like?"

Sam was already at the drinks table.

"I very rarely drink midday. But could I have a very small sherry?"

"But of course," Sam said, his mouth twitching in a faint smile.

Peter Brewster showed up some time after Sam had finished his afternoon cup of tea. He had met the out-of-town rush as he reached the outskirts of London and been delayed.

"Hello, Mr Brewster. Good of you to come."

"You said it was urgent."

"Yes. Please come in."

"Has something happened?" Brewster strode quickly into the flat, his manner agitated. "Is it something to do with Jill?"

"No, no. How is she, by the way?"

"She seems much better. She's relieved now that she finally decided to tell you the truth. I only wish to goodness she'd confided in you earlier."

"I want to ask a favour of you, Mr Brewster, but before I tell you what it is, I have to finish this phone call. So if you'll excuse me?"

"Yes, of course."

"I've been trying all afternoon to get hold of my father's lawyer. A most elusive character. I must have telephoned his office at least half a dozen times in the past hour. Please — do help yourself to a drink."

"May I have a Scotch?"

"Yes, of course."

Sam smiled and picked up the telephone.

"George? Sorry about that. Now about this notebook..."

It was late that night when Sam let George Adams out of the flat. Instead of going straight back into the sitting-room he went into the small cloakroom opening off the hall. He did not turn the light on. The opaque window was slightly open. Through it he could look down into the street. He saw George Adams emerge onto the pavement below — a well-groomed figure in his dark coat, with a briefcase tucked under his arm. The lawyer crossed the road and unlocked the door of his Rover. He started the engine up and drove off.

When the car disappeared the square seemed deserted. The gates of the park opposite had been locked at sundown. Patches of light from the street lamps fell on the mown grass. The usual selection of dark, anonymous cars was parked along the park railings. Half a dozen were on the yellow line in front of the houses where parking was restricted by day. From this angle Sam could not see whether there was anyone sitting in them or not. Further along an unblinking red light indicated that the workmen who had taken the pavement up had still not finished their job.

Sam went back to the sitting-room. The trap was now baited. Unless all his calculations were wrong he could soon expect a visit from the person who had adopted the code-name of Hogarth.

He left the doors leading to his bedroom and the hall ajar, switched out all the lights except the standard lamp behind the chair which he always sat in when reading. He placed a leather-bound notebook bearing his father's initials on the low table beside it. Then he selected a copy of *Born Free* from his book-case and settled down in the chair.

There was no knowing how long he would have to wait.

The church clock across the square chimed the half-hour, then three quarters. Sam was still reading and listening. From the back of the house somewhere came a faint metallic tremor, as if the bass string of a giant harp

185

had been very gently plucked. The sound was quickly masked by the diesel engine of a taxi passing below.

In the kitchen the tap with the worn washer was dripping persistently. The noise seemed to get louder and louder as his ears became more sharply attuned to the silence. As the church clock chimed the four quarters and began to strike eleven he heard a faint swish from his bedroom, reminiscent of the sound of an ice-skater making a turn. Still, he did not move.

The shrilling of the front doorbell, even though he was expecting it, made him start. He picked the notebook up and put it in his pocket. Then he stood up and went out to the hall.

The bell rang again as Sam opened the door.

"Oh, Mr Harvey, I don't know what you'll think of me coming at this time of night, but I have to see you. Something extraordinary has happened. Thank goodness you weren't in bed!"

"You'd better come in, Margaret." He glanced quickly down the stairs as he opened the door for her. There was no-one else in sight.

"You may wonder why I didn't phone," she said, "but I felt I had to see you, to talk to you personally."

Margaret was standing, clutching her handbag, her eyes wide, her cheeks paler than usual.

"Come on in," he said again.

She came forward hesitantly, looking behind her as she did so. Even when he had closed the door she stood rooted to the floor.

"What's happened, Margaret? You look as if you'd seen a ghost."

"I'll be all right in a minute — "

"What you need is a drink."

He led the way into the sitting-room. On the threshold

186

he stopped dead. Walter Randell, his hair dishevelled and his suit much the worse for negotiating the fire-escape and climbing through the window, was standing in the middle of the room. He had a stiletto in his hand, a duplicate of the one Sam had seen sticking out of Phil Morgan's back.

"Into the room," a voice said behind him. It was hardly recognisable as Margaret Randell's.

He turned round. She had not made the same mistake as Voss, but was standing well back from him. The automatic in her hand was small, but none the less lethal, and she looked as if she knew how to use it.

"Which of you is Mr Hogarth?" Sam said, facing Walter again.

"You can take your pick, Harvey," Walter said. "I expect you know what we've come for."

"I think I can guess. You're late. I was expecting you an hour ago."

"Where's that notebook?"

Sam moved towards him. "My dear Randell, or Hogarth or whatever you choose to call yourself, I thought you were a business man. You don't expect me to just hand the notebook over to you. The notebook contains information which is worth a great deal of money, so why on earth should I just give it to you? I suggest you bid for it. Where shall we start? Five thousand, ten thousand . . . "

"He's playing for time," Margaret said.

"Don't try and be clever," Walter warned. "Your father double-crossed me. I'd advise you not to try and emulate him."

"That's the last thing I want to do, I assure you."

"Don't waste time!" Margaret said from behind him. As he had moved forward she had come to the threshold of the room. Randell said: "You saw what happened to Morgan."

"I'm not Morgan. And let me give you a piece of friendly advice, Mr Randell. If you do decide to do anything silly, try not to lose one of your cuff-links."

"You saw the cuff-link?"

"Yes. I saw it when I came into the flat."

"Then why didn't you pick it up?"

"I was just about to when I heard Morgan groaning—"

"Morgan was dead. He was dead when I left him."

Sam shook his head, holding Walter's attention with his eyes. "He died on the way to the hospital, but not before he'd made a statement."

"He's lying, Walter," Margaret said. "He's just playing for time. Sit down in that chair, Harvey!"

Sandwiched between the gun and the stiletto Sam did not have much choice. He sat down in the upright chair.

Walter stood facing him.

"Where's the notebook belonging to your father?"

Sam said nothing.

"Try the bastard's pockets," Margaret suggested. Walter still had the stiletto in his hand. He thrust the point to within an inch of Sam's throat. His left hand groped in Sam's pockets and suddenly produced the notebook. The needle-sharp point of the stiletto touched Sam's skin. Walter crammed the notebook into his own pocket. Then he thrust his face close to Sam's. For once the spectacles did not need adjusting. The expression in his eyes was not kindly.

"Now, Harvey, let's see how you—"

Sam never found out whether he would have buried the blade in his throat. From the direction of the hall came a faint metallic scraping sound.

"There's someone at the front door!" Margaret shouted. "Let's go, Walter!"

Walter had passed out of his field of vision. He heard

them move to the door of his bedroom, could visualise Margaret backing away with the gun trained on him. He did not move.

Then the bedroom door slammed. He unclasped his hands and swivelled round. He did not get up, but sat there awaiting developments. There was a faint smile on his face.

After perhaps ten seconds the bedroom door was flung open again and Margaret re-appeared closely followed by her husband. As they rushed through the sitting-room Sam knew that this was the most dangerous moment he had to face. Margaret, her face twisted, swung the gun in his direction. He dived sideways behind the cover of the desk. A bullet smashed into the wood.

He heard their footsteps as they hurried through the hall and the sound of the front door opening. Then there was a sudden cessation of movement.

A familiar voice said: "Good evening, Mr Randell. May we detain you for a moment?"

Sam scrambled up and looked across the desk. Margaret and Walter were slowly backing away from the front door. The figure of Bellamy, awe inspiring in his moment of triumph, stalked after them. At his shoulders were two constables in uniform. No weapons were in evidence, yet Margaret had already dropped the gun.

As Walter Randell and Margaret retreated into the sitting-room the sergeant and constable who had come up the fire-escape walked through the bedroom door.

"You took your time, Bellamy," Sam said, feeling the place where the point of the stiletto had nicked his skin.

That was when Margaret Randell found her voice. The ladylike mask had disappeared.

Sam listened to the flood of abuse for half a minute before he could get a word in.

189

"Really, Margaret! Your language! For such a private kind of person you have a remarkable vocabulary."

Bert Sinclair's office was unnaturally tidy. Now that the Marius of Rye case had been solved all the material connected with it had been classified and taken away to the department which would deal with the prosecution. The neat desk awaited the next case which would land in the Chief Superintendent's lap.

The secretary who had brought in the two cups of coffee gave Sam a smile and withdrew. Sam took his cup and sat down in the easy chair. Bert leant against his desk, stirring the four lumps of sugar he had put in his cup.

"We've found the two cars, Sam. MKO 623P and SUX 876M. Your father had hidden them in a warehouse on the Slough trading estate, obviously with the intention of picking them up later. The customs people are delighted. They've already seized two hundred kilos of cannabis resin and we haven't discovered the third car yet."

Sam did not appear to share Bert's elation. He nodded gloomily and sipped his coffee.

"I'm sorry, Sam," Bert said, his tone changing. "About your parents, I mean. We all are. I only hope the media don't make a meal of it."

"I'm convinced in my own mind that my mother knew absolutely nothing about Jason's activities. Certainly not until they reached London Airport. Then, I'm afraid, it was the old story. 'What's good enough for Jason is good enough for Hannah'."

Bert observed a short silence before putting the question that was on his mind.

"What made you suspect that Walter and Margaret Randell were working together?"

"Early on I had an uneasy feeling about them. There

was a little too much emphasis on their mutual dislike of each other. Also I could not understand why 'Hogarth' had not broken into Pennymore. After all, it was Jason's notebook he was looking for. Then I realised that if Randell was Hogarth there was no need for him to break into the house. Margaret Randell had a key. She was able to search the house from top to bottom at her leisure. She and Randell realised that they'd slipped up on this and rather late in the day they invented a story about the house being searched."

"But you still suspected the Morrises and Peter Brewster."

"I could not eliminate them. That's why I had to put on that charade about telephoning George Adams."

Bert Sinclair decided his coffee was not sweet enough. He took two more lumps from the bowl and began to stir the mixture again.

"According to Bellamy there was quite a feud going on at one time between Walter Randell and Chris Morris."

"Yes. Randell had threatened to sue Chris over an article she'd written. In the end he had to back down but he swore he'd get even with her one day."

"That's why they invented the story about the boy."

"Yes. And don't forget about the sketches which were copies of Hubert's work; it was a clever touch to fake up a Marius of Rye carrier bag. But let's face it, Randell had one piece of bad luck."

"The cuff-link?"

"Yes. It must have got broken in the struggle with Morgan. He realised it was in the flat somewhere and he told his wife to go and look for it. She saw it as soon as she entered the hall — but not before I'd seen it and not before one of the residents had seen her leaving the building."

Bert looked up as there came a knock on the door. A uniformed sergeant entered. He was carrying a sheet of A4 paper covered with closely typewritten lines. He handed it to Bert and went out again.

Bert gave it a quick glance and then grinned across the desk at Sam.

"Another memo from Bellamy?" Sam suggested.

"Yes. It's the third this morning."